ILLUMINATION

SING 2

Sing 2 © 2021 Universal City Studios LLC. All Rights Reserved.
Published in the United States by Random House Children's Books,
a division of Penguin Random House LLC, 1745 Broadway, New York,
NY 10019, and in Canada by Penguin Random House Canada Limited,
Toronto. Random House and the colophon are registered trademarks
of Penguin Random House LLC.

rhcbooks.com

ISBN 978-0-593-37900-4 (trade) — ISBN 978-0-593-37901-1 (ebook)
Printed in the United States of America
10 9 8 7 6 5 4 3 2 1

ILLUMINATION PRESENTS

SING 2

WITHDRAWN

The Junior Novelization

Adapted by David Lewman

Random House 🏠 New York

Onstage at the New Moon Theater, the show was going well. The cast members were singing and dancing their hearts out. They all wanted this performance to be outstanding, since someone very important was in the audience.

Backstage, Buster Moon, the optimistic koala in charge of the theater, pulled back a side curtain for a quick peek.

"So," Rosita, a pig in the cast, asked anxiously, "is she here?"

Buster smiled and nodded. "There. See the dog in the middle of the third row? That's her. She's supposed to be the best talent scout in show business." All the actors backstage crowded around

Buster, trying to see how the scout was reacting to their show.

"I can't tell if she's enjoying it," said Meena, a young elephant with a beautiful singing voice.

"Come on," Buster said, stepping away from the curtain. "Let's get a better view."

While other animals sang onstage, Buster led Rosita, Meena, a gorilla named Johnny, and another pig, Gunter, onto a platform. Buster pulled a lever, and the platform rose into the catwalk high above the stage. They stepped onto it, and from there they could clearly see the whole theater—backstage, onstage, and the entire audience.

Miss Crawly, an elderly iguana with a glass eye, was already perched on the catwalk with a telescope, spying on the talent scout.

"And how are we doing up here, Miss Crawly?" Buster asked, keeping his voice low.

She handed him a clipboard with a photo of the scout and a handwritten tally of her reactions. "Oh, very good," Miss Crawly answered. "So far, I've counted nine smiles, two belly laughs, and five chuckles . . . though the last one could've just been gas."

In the audience, the talent scout, whose name was Suki Lane, stared at the stage with an expression on her face that was hard to read.

"Well, that's proof, right?" Buster said, studying the clipboard. "She must like the show."

"Oh my gosh," Meena said, excited. "Do you think so?"

"I hope so," Rosita said. They all hoped the talent scout would love their show and recommend that it move to Redshore City, where people came from all over the world to be entertained.

"She'd be, like, cuckoo not to love ziss show!" Gunter insisted in his European accent.

"All right, now, keep up the good work," Buster coached. "Come on, everybody—back to your positions." He herded them onto the platform again so they could ride down to the stage. "Dream big dreams," he called down from the catwalk. "That's what I've always said, right?"

"Mmm-hmm," Miss Crawly agreed, still watching the scout through her telescope.

"Well, looks like we're about to take this show to the entertainment capital of the world!" Buster predicted enthusiastically.

Then Miss Crawly looked up from the telescope, worried. "Mr. Moon, she's leaving!"

"Huh?" Buster said. Why would the scout be leaving already? The show wasn't even half over!

"She's leaving the show!" Miss Crawly exclaimed.

"Miss Crawly, stay right here!" Buster ordered.

"What are you gonna do?" the iguana asked.

Buster climbed up to a trolley dangling from a wire. "I'm gonna follow that dog!" he explained as he zipped away, riding the wire like a zip line over the audience and through a gap in the back wall, ending up right over a balcony box. He dropped into a comfy chair next to the box's only occupant, Nana Noodleman. In her glory days, she'd been a famous singer, but now she was a grandmotherly sheep who supported the performances of younger singers and dancers.

"Good heavens!" she cried, surprised to see Buster drop in.

"Hey, Nana!" Buster said.

"What *are* you doing?" she asked.

"The scout is leaving!" he explained.

Nana peered over the edge of her box. "Ah. So she is," she said. "Hurry!"

Buster rushed to the theater's front lobby, where he spotted Suki Lane looking at her phone. He flew down the stairs to intercept her. "Uh, Suki?" he said, a little out of breath. "Suki Lane?"

Still looking at her phone, the talent scout kept walking toward the exit without acknowledging Buster's existence.

"I'm Buster Moon," he said. "Uh, hi. So glad you could make it. Um, would you like some popcorn?" He grabbed a carton of popcorn from the concession stand and offered it to her.

"Oh, no thanks," Suki said. "I'm not staying for the second half, so—"

"Oh, but we thought you were enjoying it," Buster said. "I mean, not that we were watching you or anything . . ."

"It really is a cute little show," Suki admitted. "Just not what we're looking for." She headed toward the exit and through the doors.

"But . . . but wait," Buster said, following her out onto the sidewalk. "You gotta see the second act. It's a smash!"

Suki stopped and turned back to face the eager koala. "Okay, Mr. Moon," she sighed. "Can I be honest?"

"Of course."

"Are you sure?" Suki asked, raising her eyebrows and cocking her head. "Because folks say that when they don't really mean it."

"No, please," Buster insisted. "Please be as honest as you like."

"You're not good enough," Suki said bluntly.

2

Buster felt as though he'd been smacked in the face. "*What?*"

"TAXI!" Suki shouted, raising an arm. She turned back and took the carton of popcorn from Buster. "You know, maybe I will have that popcorn."

A taxi pulled up. Suki opened the back door and climbed in. But before she closed the door, she looked at Buster and said, "Look, you've got a nice little local theater here and it's great for what it is. But trust me—you'd never make it in the big leagues. Bye, now."

VROOM! The taxi pulled away from the curb.

"Well? What did she say?" a voice asked.

Buster wheeled around and saw Nana standing right behind him. "I'll be right back!" he cried, rushing off.

Inside the taxi, Suki munched on popcorn and

spoke into her phone between bites. "Nah . . . no . . . a few laughs and a bunch of quirky ideas, but definitely not for us. So, about next Thursday—"

TAP! TAP! TAP!

Suki looked and was amazed to see Buster tapping on the cab window! He was cycling alongside the taxi. "Oh, my . . ." she groaned.

"Yeah, hi!" Buster said brightly. "It's me again!"

"I'll call you back," Suki said into her phone. She lowered the window. "Are you out of your mind?"

Buster ignored her question. "When are you holding auditions?" he asked.

"Well, tomorrow," Suki admitted. "But there is no way—"

HONK! A driver passing Buster yelled, "Get out of the road, you idiot!"

"Hey, do you mind?" Buster yelled back. "I'm in a meeting here!" He turned back to Suki. "Could you at least give us a chance to try out for your boss?"

Suki pressed the button to raise the window and said to the driver, "Could you please lose this maniac?"

The taxi sped up and swerved. Buster launched over a wall and into a canal. *SPLASH!* He disappeared under the water . . . but then surfaced on the back of a whale! *FWOOSSHHHH!* The whale blasted air out its blowhole, shooting Buster skyward!

SPLISH. SPLOSH. SPLISH. SPLOSH. Feeling utterly defeated, Buster plodded slowly up the steps to the New Moon Theater. He looked at the goofy poster for their show and sighed.

Inside, Buster sloshed into the restroom and hit the button on the hand dryer. *WHIRRRR!* The warm air dried him off. When he walked out of the restroom into the lobby, he looked like a giant puffball. The theater doors opened and the happy audience poured out, buzzing with compliments for the show they'd just enjoyed.

Their enthusiasm didn't cheer Buster up one bit.

Later, after everyone had left, Nana Noodleman searched the theater for Buster. "Mr. Moon?" she called. She checked behind the set and in a closet, but the koala wasn't there. Nana opened the door to his office, went in, and looked around. Buster wasn't behind the sofa. He wasn't under his desk.

Finally, she pulled open one of the desk drawers. Inside, still looking like a giant puffball, was Buster, hiding from the world.

9

"Oh, for heaven's sake," Nana said.

"What can I say, Nana?" Buster sighed. "I'm a failure."

"Oh, poppycock," she said.

"I was reaching too high," Buster concluded.

Nana shook her woolly head. "Honestly, one negative comment, and it's all 'Woe is me.'"

Buster climbed out of the drawer. "Nana, come on! She said I'm not good enough! I mean, heck, I've just been told that my destiny—all my hopes and dreams—ends right here!"

Nana shrugged. "Well, what did you expect? That she would drop to her knees and declare you a genius? 'Roll out the red carpet for the great Buster Moon!'"

"SHE RAN ME OFF THE ROAD INTO A CANAL!" Buster argued.

This information didn't seem to impress Nana at all. "Well, you're still in one piece, aren't you?"

Buster couldn't believe how unsympathetic Nana was being. "Well, yeah, but—"

"Well, anyone who dares to set out to follow their dreams is bound to face a lot worse than a dip in a canal!" Nana declared firmly. Her butler and driver, Hobbs, appeared in the office doorway. "Ah, Hobbs!

10

I found him. Bring the car around, will you? There's a good chap." Hobbs nodded and went off to fetch the car.

Buster shook his head sadly. "I just thought Suki Lane would at least see that we deserved a shot."

Nana raised her chin. "Never mind what this person you don't even know said. Do *you* think you're good enough?"

"Of course! But, but—" Buster spluttered.

"Then you must fight for what you believe in!" Nana told him. "Guts, stamina, faith—these are the things you need now! And without them? Well, maybe that scout was right." She walked toward the door. "Maybe you're *not* good enough."

Buster was stunned.

Nana left, but she snuck one last look at Buster to see how her tough words had affected him. She'd meant to give him something to think about.

And she certainly had.

3

That night, Buster couldn't sleep, thinking about what Nana had said. He tossed and turned, burying his head under his pillow.

Then he threw the pillow aside, got up, and ran out of his bedroom. He hurried down a spiral staircase to his workspace. He found a large trunk, opened it, and started packing it full of props and costumes.

Moments later, Buster was dragging the heavy trunk down the street, talking to Rosita on his phone. "No, I know, but trust me on this. It'll be totally worth it." He reached the entrance to a rock-music club. "I'm outside her place now. Can you call the others and have them meet up in half an hour? Great! Thank you!"

He opened the door and entered the club. It was small and packed with enthusiastic fans of rock music.

12

Ash, a crested porcupine, was singing on the tiny stage. When she finished, the crowd went wild, cheering and applauding. "Thank you so much!" Ash told them. "Good night!"

As she came off the stage, she spotted Buster waiting in the wings. "Moon?" she said, delighted to see her friend. "Hey!" She ran up and hugged him.

"Wow, you were great out there!" Buster enthused.

"Thanks," she said, smiling. "I gotta go back out for an encore."

As she turned toward the stage, Buster quickly asked, "What are you doing after the show?"

"Uh, nothing," Ash said.

"Well, listen," Buster said, launching into the little speech he'd prepared in his mind. "I know this is crazy-short notice, but you always said you'd come back to work with us when the time was right."

"Of course!" Ash agreed.

"Well, this is that time!" Buster said.

The club's owner, a crocodile named Rick, bumped Buster out of the way. "Here," Rick said to Ash flatly. "Paycheck."

Getting shoved aside didn't stop Buster from trying to convince Ash to rejoin his cast. "I'm getting the gang together to go audition for this huge show—"

"Just a second," Ash interrupted, looking at her paycheck. "Hey, Rick!" she called to the crocodile. "How come you're only paying me half of what the other acts get?"

Rick shrugged. "I pay what I think you're worth, sweetheart."

Ash's eyes narrowed. "Oh, okay. See, I have this rule about not letting guys like you tell me what I'm worth. So unless I get paid like everyone else, I'm out of here."

Laughing, Rick said, "This is the only club in town. Where else are you going to play?"

"I have no idea," Ash admitted. "But I'm sure as heck not sticking around here." She turned her back on the crocodile and walked toward Buster. "Let's go." As she passed Buster, heading for the exit, he scrambled after her, dragging his big trunk.

"Whoa, whoa!" Rick called after them. "Wait a minute! You gotta do the encore! Hey! Ash!"

"Deal with it, *sweetheart*!" Ash called over her shoulder. She and Buster ran off into the night.

14

At the bus station, the other cast members had gathered, responding to calls from Rosita. Buster and Ash ran up to join them just as the bus driver was announcing their departure for Redshore City.

"Redshore City! The bus to Redshore City is now leaving!"

"Okay," Buster said, a little out of breath. "I got the tickets! Anyone seen Miss Crawly? Here's your ticket, Johnny."

Johnny was a young gorilla with a British accent who loved singing. But right at this moment, he didn't look very enthusiastic about Buster's big plan. "Mr. Moon," he said, hesitating. "I'm sorry, but I'm really having second thoughts about this."

"What?" Buster said, surprised. "No, no, no, wait!"

"All right, last call!" the driver barked. "Let's go!"

Meena stepped forward and said shyly, "Johnny's right. I mean, that theater scout didn't think we were good enough."

"She sounds like a jerk," Ash scoffed.

"Yah, total jerk," Gunter agreed.

Buster shook his head. "She was wrong. Dead wrong! There's a reason our show is sold out every night! And I'm telling you, her boss is going to love it!"

Gunter saw an opportunity to suggest something he'd been thinking about. "Ooh! Or maybe we could just, like, do a different show, you know?"

Buster raised a hand to quiet the excited pig. "Gunter, please. I've got this."

"Seriously!" Gunter continued. "I haff ziss idea for, like, a *space* musical!"

HONK! HONK! The impatient driver shouted through the open door of the bus, "All right! That's it! We're rolling out of here!"

"You don't want to hear about the space musical?" Gunter asked.

WHOOSH! The door closed. *VROOM!* The bus started driving away.

"Guys, come on!" Buster cried, running after the bus. "Wait!"

SCREECH! The driver slammed on the brakes. Someone had stepped right in front of the bus to stop it . . .

. . . Rosita!

She walked around from the front of the bus to lecture her fellow cast members. "Listen, you guys! I have dreamed of performing in Redshore City since I was a little kid! And besides, I just convinced my husband to babysit for the next twenty-four hours, and I am not going to waste an opportunity like that. So come on! We've got nothing to lose!"

Full of determination, the little pig turned and knocked on the door of the bus. *WHOOSH!* The door opened, and Rosita climbed on.

Buster led the rest of the cast onto the bus. As they settled into the empty seats toward the back, he handed a script to Ash. "Here," he said. "You come in on page two."

Taken aback, Ash said, "Wait—we're gonna rehearse the show here? At the back of the bus?"

"Yes, we are!" Buster answered.

"Of course we are," Johnny laughed.

"Yep!" Buster said. "We gotta get this show in the best shape ever." As the bus pulled out of the station, he saw someone coming down the aisle carrying a box stacked high with cups of coffee. "Ah, Miss Crawly! You made it! You are an angel. We're sure gonna need that coffee!"

Miss Crawly lowered the box, revealing her amazing

outfit: a flashy dress with padded shoulders, a wig, high heels, and lots of makeup.

"Whoa!" Buster exclaimed when he saw the iguana.

"Well, you did say dress to impress," Miss Crawly explained.

The bus drove out of town and through the dark desert, and the cast rehearsed their show all night. Each of them wore part of a costume or held a prop to suggest the characters they were playing. As they sang the show's songs, other passengers nodded along to the rhythm.

The next morning, Buster was still making adjustments. "Let's cut that line and have you play the guitar part through the whole scene."

"Got it," Ash said, marking her script.

Meena was staring out the window. She turned to her fellow performers and said excitedly, "Guys! We're here!"

They all rushed to the windows and saw the gleaming high-rise hotels, theme-park roller coasters, fountains, and monorails of Redshore City. With the sunlight reflecting off the glass and polished steel of the buildings, it looked like the most exciting city in the world!

The bus dropped off Buster and his cast right in front of the Crystal Corporation Building, a huge skyscraper where the famous showbiz mogul Mr. Crystal presented his spectacular shows. They craned their necks to peer up at the magnificent glass-and-steel building. "All right," Buster said. "Let's go spread a little Moon Theater magic."

They all cheered! This was it! THE BIG TIME!

Inside, they found their way to a receptionist sitting behind a long desk in a vast, modern lobby. Buster asked to see Mr. Crystal.

"No," the receptionist said coolly.

"No?" Buster said, confused. "What do you mean, 'no'?"

"No appointment, no entry," she explained.

Buster just stood there, trying to think of the perfect thing to say that would get them in for an audition with the legendary mogul.

"Sir," the receptionist said when she saw he wasn't leaving, "do I need to call security?"

Rosita tugged Buster's arm. "We should go."

"Yes, you should," the receptionist agreed.

The cast members slunk away, defeated.

"Aw, man," Johnny said.

"Oh, I don't like ziss," Gunter said.

But Buster was listening to the receptionist talk to an orangutan who had approached the desk as they walked away.

"Hi, how may I help you?" the receptionist asked the ape politely.

"I'm here to see Mr. Crystal for the presentation," the orangutan answered. "I've got an appointment."

The receptionist checked a list and nodded. "Take the elevators to the one-hundred and eighty-seventh floor."

Now Buster knew which floor the auditions were on.

"Zis is so unfair," Gunter continued. "She's, like, totally unfair, zat lady."

"I mean, why's she gotta be so snotty about it?" Ash asked.

"I got all dressed up for nothing," Miss Crawly complained.

"Let's just find somewhere for lunch and hang out," Johnny suggested.

But suddenly, Buster pushed everybody through a door labeled MAINTENANCE. "Everyone in here!" he hissed. "Quick! Get in!"

The receptionist peered down the long lobby to

make sure Buster and his cast had left. The lobby was empty.

Inside the dark maintenance room, Buster paced, thinking.

"It's so dark in here!" Gunter whined. "What's going on?"

"Shhh!" Buster hushed. "I gotta think, I gotta think, I gotta think. I've got to think!" He found the light switch and snapped the lights on.

Meena started to pant. "Mr. Moon," the elephant said, gasping for air, "I'm not so good in small spaces."

"Ow!" Gunter yelped. "Somebody stepped on my trotter!"

"Sorry, sorry," Ash quickly said.

Buster scanned the room, looking for inspiration. He saw lots of cleaning products and a big floor polisher—the kind that janitors drove slowly down hallways. Then, on the wall, he saw a framed photo of the Employee of the Month—a male elephant! Next to the picture, a huge pair of overalls hung from a hook.

"Aha!" Buster cried, grabbing the overalls. "Meena! Aren't these overalls kind of your size?"

Meena's eyes widened.

5

WHIRRRRZZZ . . .

When she heard the sound, the receptionist looked up and saw the floor polisher slowly moving toward her desk. Meena was driving it, disguised in the janitor's overalls and cap, with a black brush serving as a mustache. Would her disguise fool the receptionist?

"Hey, Ricky," the receptionist said in a bored voice as the polisher drove slowly by. Meena's disguise had worked!

"Hi," Meena said, trying to make her voice as deep as possible.

The other cast members were clinging to the other side of the floor polisher, where the receptionist couldn't see them. They all wore overalls that didn't fit them very well.

But the receptionist didn't notice, turning her attention back to the phone to answer a call. "Crystal Entertainment," she said.

Because Buster and his friends were all on one side of the polisher, it started to tip over!

"Oh, no," Meena said quietly. "No, no, no . . ."

"Everybody hold on!" Buster whispered.

Miss Crawly dipped so low that her glass eye touched the floor, rolling in its socket like a wheel. Somehow they reached the elevators without the receptionist noticing them. They jumped off the floor polisher and hurried toward an elevator that was heading up.

"Good job!" Buster said. "Now, into the elevator! Quick! Go, go, go!"

They all piled into one elevator, squishing up against each other. Just before she got on, Meena grabbed a bunch of mops off the floor cleaner. They all squeezed in and the doors closed.

"We could get arrested for this," Rosita said, worried about passing themselves off as janitors.

WHOOSH! The elevator rocketed up to the 187th floor. *DING!* The doors slid open, and Buster saw a large room full of performers silently waiting to audition, all of them staring at the elevator crammed full of janitors wearing overalls that didn't fit.

"Everybody mop," Buster whispered, and they mopped their way out of the elevator, across the waiting area, and down the hall, out of sight.

DING! Another elevator arrived. The doors opened, and three sophisticated giraffes got off. But as soon as their shoes hit the wet, newly mopped floor, they skittered, slipped, and fell. *WHAM! WHAM! WHAM!*

Buster led the way down a corridor.

"Where are you going now?" Rosita asked.

"We gotta find somewhere to change out of these overalls," Buster explained, trying to open some doors. The first two were locked, but the third one was open. Buster waved everybody inside, following them in and closing the door.

They found themselves backstage in a huge auditorium. As the others changed out of the overalls into their audition costumes, Buster peeked through a thick curtain. In the audience, he saw a white wolf surrounded by assistants. He realized the wolf must be Mr. Crystal, the owner of the building and the person who would decide whether the New Moon Theater troupe members were good enough to perform in Redshore City.

At that moment, Mr. Crystal was watching two cows dance and sing onstage. Buster beckoned to his performers.

"Look," he whispered. "That's him. That is *the* Mr. Crystal." Everyone hurried over to peek through the curtain at the wolf holding their fates in his hands.

As the cows sang, Mr. Crystal frowned. He growled, "Garbage," and pressed a button. A loud buzzer told the auditionees they'd been rejected. *BZZZZZT!*

One after another, performers were quickly cut off by Mr. Crystal. Three little chicks singing as they popped out of chimneys on a set. *BZZZZZT!* Two chimpanzees and a turtle doing a magic trick. *BZZZZZT!* A bunny serenading a hippo. *BZZZZZT!* A horse in an elegant gown singing with great emotion. *BZZZZZT!* Six herons pounding on huge drums. *BZZZZZT!* Hogs dancing a ballet. *BZZZZZT!* A slug in a hoodie singing a song about getting a call as he crawled across a phone. *BZZZZZT!*

Fifty flamingoes on roller skates sang and danced in perfect patterns. Buster was impressed (and a little intimidated), but Mr. Crystal hit his button. *BZZZZZT!*

Mr. Crystal's assistant, a cat named Jerry, ushered

the pink birds off the stage. "Okay, everybody, if you can leave immediately, single file, we'd appreciate that. Thank you very much."

Sighing with disappointment, the flamingoes slunk off the stage and left the cavernous theater.

"Well, where's the next group, Jerry?" Mr. Crystal barked from the audience. "Why am I sitting here waiting?"

"Oh, I just," Jerry stammered nervously. "I just, uh—"

"Be useful or be gone," Mr. Crystal warned his assistant.

"Yes, sir!" Jerry said, looking around frantically for the next act. He spotted Buster peeking through the curtains. "Hey, you! Yeah, you! Little guy! You're here for the audition?"

"Uh, yes. Yes, we are," Buster answered. He turned to the members of his troupe and hissed, "Guys! We're on! Right now!"

"Now?" Meena gulped, caught off guard.

"What?" Johnny asked at the same time.

It was now or never.

6

Shaking with nerves, the cast members hurried onstage with their props and costumes.

"Your name?" Jerry asked Buster.

"It's Buster Moon," he said. "From the New Moon Theater." He looked out into the audience to address Mr. Crystal. "And we're very excited to share our story with you today, sir."

"Yeah, great," Mr. Crystal said, unimpressed. "Now get to it."

"Of course!" Buster said, nodding eagerly. "Yes." He turned to his friends. "Okay, guys, just like we rehearsed it."

Miss Crawly hit Play on a boombox, and their music started. Meena and Johnny stepped forward. Over the music, Buster solemnly narrated, "This is the story of an ordinary high school girl who discovers—"

BZZZZZT!

"Stop!" Mr. Crystal ordered.

"Stop?" Buster asked, confused. They'd barely started!

"He wants you to stop," Jerry clarified unnecessarily.

Miss Crawly stopped the music. The cast paused, not sure what to do.

Shaking his head, Mr. Crystal said, " 'Ordinary' and 'school'—two words I will never be associated with."

"Never," Jerry echoed for emphasis, "never."

Mr. Crystal turned to his assistant. "Where the heck did you dig these guys up from?"

Jerry tried to rush the New Moon Theater crew out. "If you could all leave very quickly, we'd appreciate that. Please."

"I need big shows, Jerry!" Mr. Crystal shouted. "Big ideas!"

"Yes, sir!" Jerry agreed. "Big! The biggest!"

Gunter stepped forward, raising his hand. "Hey! I haff a big one!"

"Okay, honey," Rosita said, taking Gunter by the arm and trying to lead him off the stage. "Come on. Let's go."

Looking at Buster, Gunter continued speaking. "You know, the sci-fi musical! Dat's big, right?"

Mr. Crystal looked slightly intrigued. Encouraged, Gunter went on. "I mean, it's got za aliens and za robots and za lasers and zees amazing songs from, like, Clay Calloway—"

"Whoa, Clay Calloway?" Mr. Crystal interrupted. "I love Clay Calloway!"

The second he heard this, Buster jumped in. "I know, right? I mean, doesn't everybody?"

Mr. Crystal stood up and moved closer to the stage. "Yeah, see, Jerry? This is exactly the kind of big idea I'm talking about."

"Yes, sir!" Jerry said, always quick to agree with his boss.

Mr. Crystal asked Buster, "So, what's this show of yours called?"

"What's it called?" Buster said, having no idea. He turned to Gunter. "Gunter? You want to tell Mr. Crystal what the show is called?"

Thinking fast, Gunter said, "It's called . . . *Out of Ziss World!*"

Nodding and thinking, Mr. Crystal repeated the title to himself, liking the sound of it. *"Out of This World . . ."*

"That's right," Buster said. "Just imagine it!" He signaled to Ash, who started playing a Clay Calloway song on her guitar. "A spectacular musical that takes your audience out of this world!"

Ash sang the famous songwriter's lyrics. Soon Johnny joined in, and so did the rest of the cast.

Picturing stars and planets, Mr. Crystal said in awe, "I love this song."

But the imagined show was interrupted when his talent scout Suki Lane entered, saying, "Sir, your lunch meeting . . ." When she saw everyone from the New Moon Theater, she gasped and stopped in her tracks. "Oh, my."

"Not now!" Mr. Crystal snapped, angered by the interruption.

"Moon?" said Suki. "How did you get in here?"

Ignoring her, Mr. Crystal walked up to Buster. "Are you telling me you got Clay Calloway's permission to use his songs?"

"Well," Buster countered, "what if I told you I did?" He figured that wasn't a lie. Just a little misleading.

"Oh, okay," Mr. Crystal said, taking Buster's answer as a yes. "So, you got some kind of personal connection to this guy?"

Buster hesitated a second, but then said, "How else would I get his permission?"

Ash tried to get Buster's attention, frantically whispering, "Moon!"

But Mr. Crystal didn't notice Ash's efforts, because a tremendous idea had just occurred to him. "Wait, if you know him, then you could get him to be in the show, right? That'd be huge for me and my theater. Huge!"

Suki stepped forward. "Sir, I'm sorry to interrupt, but . . . seriously? You think this little guy from nowhere can get Clay Calloway in the show?"

That made Buster mad. He puffed out his koala chest and said, "Well, Suki, for your information, I am not just a little guy from nowhere." With a steely look of determination in his eye, he turned to Mr. Crystal and said confidently, "Consider it done, sir."

Seconds later, the doors from the theater to the waiting area banged open. *BLAM!* Mr. Crystal marched briskly through, followed by Buster, his cast, Suki, and Jerry. "I'll give you three weeks, Moon," Mr. Crystal announced. "Three weeks to get this show up and running, okay?"

"Yes, sir!" Buster said happily. "Thank you!"

As Mr. Crystal marched off, Ash said, "Moon, do you really know Clay Calloway?"

"Shhh," Buster said. "Not now!"

Moments later, they were all up on the skyscraper's roof. As he headed toward his waiting helicopter, Mr. Crystal snapped orders at Jerry. "I want these guys to start work right away. Set them up with our designers, our dancers—whatever they need. And get them rooms at the hotel, okay? The very best suites. The whole shaboodle."

"Yes, sir," Jerry said, writing notes on a clipboard. "Yes, of course."

Mr. Crystal stopped. "One last thing." He leaned down to stare Buster in the face. "Don't you ever do anything to make me look bad. You got that?"

"Oh, I will never let that happen, sir!" Buster vowed.

"You'd better not," Mr. Crystal warned, "or I'll throw you off the roof."

7

Buster laughed, assuming Mr. Crystal was joking.

But the wolf stared at him menacingly. Then he climbed into the helicopter, calling, "Great job, everyone!" He turned to the pilot. "Take it away, Raoul!" The chopper lifted off, blowing a stiff wind with its blades.

"Oh my gosh!" Rosita said excitedly. "Is this really happening?"

"Yah!" Gunter exclaimed. "We're playing Redshore City, baby!"

Everyone cheered.

Buster patted Gunter on the back, congratulating him for coming up with his big idea. "Gunter! Sci-fi musical? You're a genius!"

Gunter grinned. "Well, Mama alvays said, 'Gunter, you're not as stupid as your papa!'"

"No, you're not!" Buster agreed. The thrilled koala spotted Suki, who did not look happy. He walked over to her. "Hey, Suki, no hard feelings, huh?"

"You have no idea what you're getting into," she told him before turning on her heel and walking out.

Ash yanked Buster aside, concerned. "Are you out of your mind?"

"What?" Buster asked.

"Clay Calloway?" Ash said in disbelief. "I'm, like, his biggest fan, and I can tell you, the guy is a recluse! Since his wife died, no one's seen him in over fifteen years."

"Ah," Buster said. "That's not so good."

"No, it's not," Ash agreed.

Buster thought hard. He had to reach Clay Calloway somehow and get him to agree to let them use his songs in their show. And to be in the show! Otherwise, Mr. Crystal might throw him off the roof!

"Miss Crawly," he said, hurrying over to the iguana. "I need you to help me find Clay Calloway. An address, a phone number—anything. But we've got to find him."

"Yes, sir!" Miss Crawly said, saluting.

The next morning, Nana Noodleman sat propped up on satiny pillows in her elegant bed watching TV. Hobbs opened the bedroom curtains, letting sunlight pour in from the windows. As he set a breakfast tray down in front of his employer, he noticed her smiling at the television. Curious to see what was amusing her, he glanced at the screen and saw a horse named Linda Le Bon presenting the news. Next to her was a photo of Buster Moon!

"What?" Hobbs asked, surprised to see the little koala from the theater on the news.

Nana just kept smiling, pleased that Buster had gone to Redshore City, auditioned, and won his chance at the big time. She sipped her tea, satisfied with herself for challenging him to not give up.

That day, limousines carried Buster and his cast to the Crystal Tower Hotel. Before they could open the car doors themselves, their drivers rushed around to do it for the happy passengers. When Mr. Crystal had ordered Jerry to make sure the New Moon Theater

36

players got "the whole shaboodle," he'd meant it!

They weren't even allowed to carry their own luggage. Bellhops dressed in splendid uniforms hurried to load their bags and instruments onto carts and whisk them away to the luxury suites that had been reserved for them. As Buster and his friends entered the hotel, they were dazzled by the sight of splashing fountains and beautiful decorations. The lobby was absolutely magnificent, with soaring ceilings and glass elevators silently carrying guests up to the higher floors.

The New Moon Theater troupe members were in awe. As if in a dream, they checked in at the front desk, received keys to their suites, and rode the impossibly swift and smooth elevators up to the top of the skyscraper.

That evening, three bellhops pushed carts stacked high with delectable treats through illuminated doors and into Buster's spacious suite. But Buster was too busy frantically coming up with a script for *Out of This World* with Gunter to pay much attention. While the excitable pig paced around the room trying out ideas, Buster typed on his laptop as fast as he could.

37

"Okay," Gunter said. "So zis guy's coming in from zat side and it's, like, cuckoo-crazy, and zen I think we should haff, like, ziss cool alien tango scene!" He started singing a song appropriate for a tango.

Buster repeated as he typed, "Alien . . . tango . . . scene. Oh, I love it!"

"Wait!" Gunter cried, stopping and holding up his hands. "I've got a better idea. What if it was, like, a big underwater scene instead?"

"Underwater?" Buster asked. He wasn't sure it was a great idea for a live show onstage.

But Gunter was certain. "Yah, yah, I'm sure of ziss. Write it down."

"Mmm," Buster said, still not convinced. "Okay." He started to type again, but Gunter stopped him.

"Wait! Wait!" he said. "Stop your clicky-clacky! I haff a better idea!"

"You can't keep changing your mind!" Buster protested.

"Why?" Gunter asked.

"Why?" Buster said. "Because in exactly twenty minutes, the stage crew are coming here to start work on our show and we need to lock this stuff down!"

DING DONG!

The doorbell! Terrified, Buster stared at the door to his suite. "Oh my gosh. They're early!"

But Gunter just kept spouting more elaborate ideas for his space musical. "Oooh, and I want to haff, like, zis beautiful luff scene wiz, like, a duet, but za guy's frozen in ice!"

Hurrying toward the door, Buster passed Miss Crawly. "Anything on Calloway?"

She shook her head. "Not a thing."

Buster sighed. He reached the door and turned the knob. He opened the door to reveal a large group of stage-crew members.

"Ah, Mr. Moon," said the one in front, whose name was Mason, "we're your production team, and we're here to start—"

"Yes, yes, yes," Buster interrupted nervously, stepping out into the hall. "You're here to work on the show, and I would gladly invite you all in right now, but—"

"We should totally do a battle scene!" Gunter announced, bursting out into the hallway.

"Gunter, no! Not now!" Buster said, pushing him back into the suite. He turned to the waiting production team, chuckling, trying to act calm and seem at ease.

"I just need a little more time to hammer out a few minor details. So would it be okay if you all could come back in, like, an hour? Or maybe four? And I really appreciate your patience." He slipped back into the suite and shut the door.

The crew members looked at each other. What was going on?

"Hmm," Mason said. "Okay."

Inside the suite, Buster wiped his brow. "Okay, that was not a great start."

Miss Crawly picked a card out of a fruit basket and read it. "Oh, look. It's a gift from Mr. Crystal."

"Oh," Buster said, pleased.

"It says, 'Don't mess up, Moon. Or else.'"

Buster's smile melted away.

8

The next morning, the whole cast and crew gathered around Buster in the gigantic auditorium theater.

"Good morning!" he said brightly. "On behalf of myself and the cast, I just want to say that to be given this incredible opportunity to work with you all here at the Crystal Tower Theater is an honor for us. I believe that together we can make a show that'll take the audience out of this world!"

He whipped the cloth off a model of the show's futuristic set. Impressed, everyone oohed and aahed.

"A big thanks to Steve for staying up all night to make this model," Buster said, gesturing toward an exhausted bloodhound. "Great work, Steve!"

Buster opened the model up for everyone to see. He took a small figure out of a spaceship and let it dangle on a wire. "And here's the star of our show . . . Rosita!"

"Ha, ha!" Gunter laughed joyfully. "That's you, baby!"

Rosita was shocked. "The lead role?"

"Trust me," Buster said, smiling. "You are perfect for it."

Laughing and clapping, the cast members hugged Rosita, thrilled for her. "Wait until my kids hear!" Rosita said, wiping away a happy tear.

"So," Buster said when they'd finished congratulating her, "the story goes like this. Rosita plays an astronaut searching for a missing space explorer. Along with her trusty robot—"

"Dat's me!" Gunter said proudly.

"—they follow the trail across four planets," Buster continued. "There's a planet of war, a planet of love, one of despair, and one of joy. Each planet will have its own spectacular musical number performed by one of our terrific cast members."

The New Moon Theater players chattered excitedly. The show sounded wonderful!

"And how does it end?" Rosita asked. "Do I find the explorer?"

"Oh, we have no idea what we're going to do at the end," Gunter admitted frankly. Hearing this, the crew members murmured with concern. How were they supposed to put a show up in three weeks if the creators didn't even know how it ended?

Buster tried to smooth things over. "Gunter, no, no, no. We do have great ideas for the ending. We just have to work on a few tiny details." He decided to change the subject. "All right! We've only got three weeks to make this a reality, folks, so let's get to work!" He turned to the young gorilla with the British accent. "Johnny, you are going to play an alien warrior in a fantastic battle scene!"

"Yes!" Johnny cried, pumping his fist.

"Come with me," Buster said, leading Johnny off the stage.

Buster showed Johnny the way to the Crystal Tower Theater's dance studio, where performers learned and practiced their routines. One wall was lined with mirrors, and a bar for dancers to hold while they stretched. When Buster and Johnny entered, a few dancers were stretching and bending their legs and bodies in ways that seemed almost impossible.

"Johnny," Buster said, "I want you to meet your fellow dancers."

"'Allo, lads," Johnny said, greeting them. He leaned

down and spoke confidentially to Buster. "I thought you said I was going to be in a battle scene."

"Well, you are," Buster explained, "but Gunter saw it as more of a dance battle."

"Ohhh-kaaay," Johnny said. He'd been excited about being in a battle scene, but he wasn't at all confident about his dancing. He thought of himself as a singer.

Buster saw Johnny frowning with concern. "Don't worry," he reassured him. "You're going to be working with the number-one choreographer in Redshore City!" He pulled a business card out of his pocket and showed it to Johnny. There was a picture of a stern-looking monkey on it.

" 'Klaus Kickenklober'?" Johnny read.

"Yep," Buster said, nodding. "Klaus'll turn you into a pro dancer in no time!"

"Okay," Johnny said, still sounding unsure about the whole dancing thing.

Meena burst into the studio just then, looking very anxious. "Mr. Moon?"

"You okay, Meena?" Buster asked, taking her off to the side.

"Gunter said I'm in a romantic scene," she said nervously. Then she whispered, "I have to kiss someone."

Buster nodded. "Yeah, it's gonna be an amazing, beautiful, romantic scene."

Keeping her voice low, Meena confided, "Mr. Moon, I've never even had a boyfriend or any of that stuff!"

"Aww, don't you worry," Buster said, giving the elephant a reassuring pat. "I'm going to cast a great partner for you."

"Promise?"

"Promise."

"Mr. Moon," Mason said, walking in with all his workers. "We're ready to start building the rest of the sets."

Buster took the foreman aside and spoke to him quietly. "Okay, listen, I don't know exactly what the rest of the sets are yet, so could you give me one more night to figure this out?"

Mason turned back to his workers and shouted, "THIS GUY DOESN'T HAVE IT FIGURED OUT, SO WE CAN'T START WORK RIGHT NOW."

Frantically patting the air with his hands, Buster tried to shush Mason. "Mason! Hey, listen, don't—"

But Mason kept shouting. "DID EVERYBODY HEAR THAT? HE DOES NOT HAVE THIS SHOW FIGURED OUT. I'M LOOKING INTO HIS EYES,

AND ALL I SEE IS FEAR AND A LITTLE BIT OF SHAME."

"Yeah, I think everyone heard you, Mason," Buster said, ushering him out. "Thank you so much." Then he looked around for his writer. "Gunter, come on. We have work to do!"

In the big hotel suite that night, Buster typed on his laptop while Gunter paced the room, coming up with more ideas for *Out of This World*.

". . . and then I'm thinking Ash can have a duet with Clay Calloway," Gunter said excitedly. "Because she's a star who's guiding them all the way back home!"

"Yes, Gunter," Buster agreed, typing as fast as he could. "That's perfect for Ash!"

BANG!

The door to the suite burst open and a crowd of piglets ran in, yelling, "MOMMY!" They scurried straight to Rosita, clambering all over her.

"Oh, my darlings!" she squealed. "You're here! I wasn't expecting you until the morning!"

Her husband, Norman, dragged a pile of luggage into the suite. Though he was exhausted, he smiled,

46

happy to see his wife. "They couldn't wait to see you," he explained. As the piglets dashed around the suite, exploring every nook and cranny, Norman made his way past his curious children to Rosita. "So, the star of the show, huh?"

"Can you believe it?" she said, grinning. "It's literally my dream come true."

"I know," Norman said before giving her a kiss. "I am so proud of you, honey."

The piglets crawled all over Buster. "Uh . . . help," he said.

"Mr. Moon!" Miss Crawly called. Buster looked and saw the iguana holding up a picture of Clay Calloway.

"I've found him!"

9

"**C**lay Calloway?" Buster asked eagerly.

"Yeah, I've found his home address!" Miss Crawly reported proudly.

"No way!" Ash said in disbelief.

"Yes way!" Buster countered. "Miss Crawly, I'm gonna need you to go visit him first thing tomorrow."

"Oh," Miss Crawly said, ready to take on this assignment. "Yes, sir."

"You'll need to rent a car and take him a letter and, uh"—Buster's gaze traveled to the big fruit basket Mr. Crystal had sent with the threatening note—"maybe that fruit basket. Yes, that fruit basket. You got that?"

Miss Crawly looked at the fruit basket with her non–glass eye. "Got it!"

The next morning, Klaus Kickenklober taught the battle number's dances to Johnny and the others in the scene. Klaus wanted everyone to do the steps exactly the way he envisioned them, and wasn't at all happy when dancers made mistakes.

". . . and one, two, three, four, five, six, seven, eight," the monkey snapped, demonstrating steps in front of the group. "We're dancing, we're dancing . . ." He froze in position. "We're holding, we're holding. Stay on point! Shuffle and hold!"

Johnny awkwardly tried to copy Klaus's moves but found it difficult. When he was supposed to freeze, he wobbled.

"I said hold!" Klaus barked, watching the dancers' reflections in the long mirror that stretched across the front wall. "Johnny, he's not holding, and one, two, three, four . . ."

"All right!" Johnny said. "I am trying!"

Klaus leaned right into Johnny's face. "Let's not forget—this is Redshore City, not your little local theater! And five, six, seven, eight!"

Johnny tried the combination of steps again.

"Ryan, that was excellent," Klaus said. "Johnny, you are doing it wrong! That was awful!"

Buster carefully danced his way through the group to Johnny, keeping in time with the frustrated gorilla. "Come on, Johnny," he said encouragingly. "You can do better."

"He's freaking me out!" Johnny admitted.

"Johnny—" Buster started to say.

"I'm trying!" Johnny insisted. Buster tried dancing alongside Johnny to encourage him, but that only made Johnny feel worse.

"And thrust!" Klaus said. "You're not thrusting, Johnny. Thrust! And thrust! Still not thrusting! Can you thrust, please?"

"Come on," Buster urged. "Thrust!"

Johnny rolled his eyes.

"Five, six, seven, and tippy-toes," Klaus continued. "Tippy-toes. I don't see your tippy-toes. Can I see those tippy-toes?"

Johnny couldn't believe Klaus was actually telling him to get up on his tippy-toes. How could this dance possibly be anything like a battle? "Oh, come on," he said. "He's havin' a laugh."

"Tippy-toes!" Buster said. "Come on. Let's go!"

50

Johnny tried to walk across the room on the tips of his toes. "That is rubbish!" Klaus criticized. "Terribly poor. Really bad."

Frustrated, Johnny stormed out of the dance studio and into the general rehearsal space. "That bloke absolutely hates me!"

Across the room, Rosita was being measured for her costume. "Hang in there, Johnny," she said soothingly. "The first week's always tough."

"Yeah, you're right," he said, plopping down next to Meena with a heavy thump.

Buster ran in looking excited. "Meena!" he called. "Come and meet your partner!"

"Oh my gosh," Meena said anxiously. "He's here?"

"Yep," Buster said. "He's called Darius. Won a ton of awards, and I think you guys are gonna have great chemistry."

But when Meena met Darius, a yak, she found him to be completely self-absorbed. He was very confident—even arrogant—bragging about all the shows he'd been in and the awards he'd won.

"My co-star," he said in the middle of a story about the last show he'd done, "was just like you, Gina. She was—"

"It's Meena," the shy elephant gently corrected.

"Excuse me?" Darius asked.

"My name," she said. "It's Meena, not Gina."

"Yeah, okay," Darius sniffed. "In the future, if you could not interrupt me, that would be way better."

When they rehearsed their duet together, Darius made big romantic gestures toward Meena. She pulled away, embarrassed.

"Oh, boy," Buster said, watching. Meena didn't look as though she even liked Darius, much less loved him. Buster knew it was going to take a lot of work. . . .

"So, where's Calloway?" Suki asked, suddenly appearing behind Buster.

"He'll be here very soon," Buster said optimistically.

"Hmm," Suki said suspiciously. "Is that so?"

"It is indeed so," Buster said, trying to sound sure of himself. "In fact, my trusty assistant, Miss Crawly, is on her way to meet him right now."

Miss Crawly drove her rental car through woods so dense and dark, she had to turn her headlights on

52

even though the sun hadn't set. Hunching over the steering wheel, she peered through the trees until she came up against a barrier made from oil barrels and barbed wire! A sign read PRIVATE PROPERTY—NO TRESPASSING!

Carrying the fruit basket and a note to Clay Calloway, Miss Crawly got out of the car and climbed over the barrier. She followed a path through the forest toward a lake, where a big, beautiful house was nestled among the trees.

Squeezing past a closed gate, Miss Crawly walked across the lawn. "Mr. Calloway! Hello! Is anybody home?" She saw no one. She also didn't see the trip wire running across the grass. When she stepped on it . . .

BANG! A shower of sparks exploded out of the ground!

WHOOO! WHOOOT! WHOOOP! Sirens wailed!

FLASH! Bright lights lit up the yard!

"WAAAHHH!" Miss Crawly screamed. Terrified, she stumbled around, tripping another wire and setting off more flares.

Next to the house, a garage door opened. Inside,

a foot pumped a pedal, firing up a mighty engine. *BRRAMMM!* A hand twisted a throttle, revving the engine. *VROOOM! VROOM!*

And then . . . *VRRRRROOOOM!* A huge motorcycle came roaring out of the garage, heading straight toward Miss Crawly!

10

The driver of the motorcycle pulled out a paint gun and fired paintballs at Miss Crawly. *SPLAT! SPLAT!* A paintball smacked into the fruit basket, blowing it apart. Fruit flew everywhere!

Screaming, Miss Crawly ran back through the woods to the barrier of oil cans and barbed wire. She leapt over the barrier and landed on the ground. *THUMP!* Her glass eye fell out and rolled away. "Okay, I gotcha," she said, feeling around for the eye. Mistaking an apple for the glass eye, she popped it into her socket and jumped into her rental car.

She didn't have room to turn around, so she put the car in reverse and started to back away. Just past the barrier, the motorcycle driver took off his helmet, revealing the handsome head of a lion.

55

Miss Crawly gasped. "Clay Calloway!"

Distracted by the sight of the elusive songwriter, Miss Crawly accidentally backed her car right into a ravine. "Oopsie-daisy!" she cried as the car went over the edge.

Back at the rehearsal hall, Buster was trying to call Miss Crawly to see how she was doing with Clay Calloway, but he only got her voice mail.

As he finished leaving a message, Buster saw Mr. Crystal and his team of assistants walk in with a young female wolf.

"Moon," Mr. Crystal said, "this is my daughter, Porsha. She wants to meet Calloway."

"I'm not expecting Clay on set just yet," Buster said, stalling. Luckily, a stagehand named Sasha called down to Buster from atop a high tower, telling him they were ready. "Excuse me," Buster apologized to Mr. Crystal and Porsha. "Rehearsal."

Up on the tower, Sasha clipped a wire to Rosita's harness. Music started, and Rosita sang along as she walked toward the end of a diving board.

"Is Mommy gonna jump off that board?" one of the piglets asked Buster.

"She sure is!" Buster said.

But before Rosita reached the edge, she felt dizzy. She looked down and saw how far it was to the stage. Panicking, she dropped down and clung to the diving board, afraid to move.

"Mr. Moon!" Gunter called. "I zink Rosita's haffing a major freak-out up here!"

"Oh, no," Buster said, rushing to the ladder that led up to the diving board.

"Hey, Moon," Mr. Crystal said, popping a snack into his mouth. "You really think the mommy pig's gonna pull this off?"

"Absolutely, sir!" Buster asserted as he climbed. "Believe me, there's nothing Rosita can't do!"

But when he reached Rosita, she whispered, "I can't do this!"

"Why didn't you tell me you were afraid of heights?" Buster asked.

"I've never been afraid before in my whole life!" Rosita said. "I don't know what happened to me!"

"Hey, you guys!" Porsha said. They turned and saw the young wolf standing at the top of the ladder. "What's going on up here?"

"Who is that?" Rosita asked.

Before Buster could answer, Porsha picked up a harness. "Oooh, can I try?"

"No, no, no," Buster said. "I can't let you jump off here."

Porsha immediately called down to her father. "Daddy! He won't let me jump!"

"Moon, come on!" Mr. Crystal said. "Let her do the thing!"

"Yay!" Porsha cheered, pulling on the harness. Before anyone could stop her, she ran and jumped off the end of the diving board, swinging through the air on the wire. "Wheeee! I love it! It's easy!"

Buster helped Rosita down the ladder. "All right, let's get you down." As they descended, Porsha kept flying back and forth. "Guys, this is exactly like the dream I had last night! You were all there! And you asked me to sing for you!" She was looking right at Buster.

"I did?" Buster asked, having no idea what to make of Porsha's dream.

"Yeah! So I did! Like this!" Porsha began to sing. Her voice was beautiful! Jerry clapped hard, never missing a chance to please his boss. The music stopped, and Porsha landed on the stage just as Buster and

Rosita reached the bottom of the ladder.

"Well, that's a lovely dream you had, there, Porsha," Buster said. He turned to everyone in the room. "Back to first positions, please. Let's try it again." He handed Rosita a helmet. "Here, Rosita. You want to try with the helmet this time?"

Porsha stepped up to Buster and Rosita. "Oh, but now I know what the dream meant!" She took the helmet from Rosita and put it on. "She's afraid, so she'll never be able to play the part. But here I am—young and not afraid at all!"

11

Buster stared at Porsha. "I can't just give you Rosita's part!"

But Mr. Crystal took Buster aside and lifted the little koala up to his face. "When an opportunity to make me happy comes along, you'd better grab it! You get me?"

Buster hesitated. He understood that Mr. Crystal wanted him to give his daughter Rosita's part, but it seemed totally unfair.

"You don't think my daughter's good enough for your show?" the mogul growled.

"No, Mr. Crystal!" Buster said. "I think she's wonderful."

"So you'll figure it out," the wolf said, putting Buster down.

"Yes, I will," Buster said. He went off to find Rosita, and Mr. Crystal left.

"Mmm-kay," Suki said, addressing the costume crew. "Let's have Porsha measured for a costume right away, please."

Buster asked Rosita if she was okay. "Maybe this is for the best," he suggested. "I mean, you really were scared up on that board."

"Right," Rosita said, nodding slowly.

"I'll write you another part, Rosita," Buster promised. "A really great part."

Rosita put on a brave face, acting as though everything were okay. But that night, alone in the hotel bathroom, she cried, heartbroken with disappointment.

The next morning, Johnny ran into the dance studio out of breath. "Sorry I'm late, Mr. Kickenklober! I was practicing and lost track of time."

"Oh," Klaus said, looking disappointed. "I thought maybe you'd had an accident and we'd never have to see you again."

"Seriously, why do you have to be so mean all the time?" Johnny asked.

61

"Because only when we suffer can we be great," Klaus said, tossing Johnny a fighting stick. "Places, everyone! Ryan, you'll be playing Johnny's opponent in the battle scene."

The music started. Johnny and Ryan circled each other, spinning their sticks. Klaus hung right behind Johnny, watching his every move. It made Johnny nervous, and he messed up.

"Sorry," Johnny told Ryan. "Sorry, sorry."

"WRONG!" Klaus shouted. "AGAIN!"

Johnny tried again, but he kept making mistakes.

"HIGHER!" Klaus screamed. "SO BAD! NO! YUCK! COME ON!"

That night, after a long day of frustrating rehearsal, Johnny rushed out of the dance studio, shaken and upset. He kicked a trash container and slammed his skateboard on the ground so hard, it broke. *SMASH!*

"Oh, man," Johnny said, picking up the pieces of his beloved board.

12

The next morning, Johnny was leaving a shop carrying a new skateboard when he heard drums. Across the street, a crowd had gathered to watch an amazing street dancer—a cat named Nooshy. When she finished, she held out her cap and people dropped money in, including Johnny.

"You're amazing!" he told her.

"Much appreciated," Nooshy said coolly.

"Listen, could I buy you a coffee or maybe something to eat?" Johnny offered.

Nooshy raised an eyebrow. "Whoa, that's a bit forward."

Shaking his head, Johnny said, "I just wanted to talk to you about maybe helping me with—"

"HEY!" a policeman yelled, pushing his way

63

through the crowd toward Nooshy. "You got a license to perform here?"

Pulling her hood up to hide her face, Nooshy told Johnny, "Actually, I'd love a chat. Let's go."

At a nearby café, Nooshy ordered a smoothie. She stuck a straw in it and started slurping it up. *SHHHLURRP!*

Johnny got right down to business. "If you could just give me some dance lessons, you would literally be saving my life."

"Wait," Nooshy said, remembering something he'd mentioned earlier. "If you're in a real show, how come you don't have a choreographer?"

Johnny rolled his eyes. "I do, but it turns out he's a massive weirdo."

Nooshy narrowed her eyes, looking at Johnny skeptically. "And how do I know you're not a weirdo? How do I know you're legit?" She sucked down more smoothie.

"Just come with me to rehearsal," Johnny answered. "See for yourself."

Shaking her head in protest, Nooshy said, "I'm not going to just follow some guy I don't know to rehearsal."

"Well, how else am I supposed to prove I'm legit?" Johnny asked, frustrated. Then he got an idea. He started to sing along with the music playing in the café. By the end of the song, everyone in the restaurant was listening and clapping along.

Nooshy grinned. "I knew you were a weirdo."

Nooshy was dazzled by the big, glittering Crystal Tower Theater, with its amazing lobby, stage, sets, props, and costumes. But when Johnny told Klaus Kickenklober that Nooshy was going to help him with his dancing, the choreographer was furious.

"You think some riffraff street dancer can help you more than me?"

"Riffraff?" Nooshy said, offended.

"Okay, hang on," Johnny said to Nooshy, calming her down. He turned to Klaus. "She's just gonna give me some extra lessons, that's all."

The monkey raised himself up to his full height. "Oh, because I, Klaus Kickenklober, master choreographer, am not good enough for Johnny!"

"No," Johnny said, holding up his hands. "That's not what I said."

"I'm irrelevant to him," Klaus went on. "I'm just a stupid, fat, old monkey!"

"I don't think that at all," Johnny said.

"I do," Nooshy said.

Johnny hushed Nooshy and turned back to Klaus. "She's only trying to help me."

"Dude," Nooshy said to Klaus, "I only need two days with him."

"Two days! Ha!" Klaus laughed. "More like two hundred years!"

"Two days," Nooshy said confidently. "He'll be amazing."

Klaus leaned close to Nooshy's face and hissed, "Oh, really? If he is, I will eat my hat."

In the theater's rehearsal space, Buster was ready to rehearse the actors. "All right," he said. "Cue the music! Lots of energy now! And . . . AAAAAAHH!"

He screamed at the sight of Miss Crawly, splattered with paint and sporting an apple where her glass eye normally was.

"Miss Crawly?" Buster said.

13

The iguana grabbed Buster by the collar. "You can't go back there, Mr. Moon! Never! Never!"

Buster couldn't stop staring at the apple in her eye socket. "What happened to you?"

"That lion!" Miss Crawly said, referring to Clay Calloway. "You see, he's crazy!" She wobbled away, muttering "Crazy! Oh, he's *crazy*!"

Watching her go, Ash said, "Wow, she's a mess!" She turned to Buster. "So, you're not going to go to Calloway's house, are you?"

"I have to," Buster said, though that was pretty much the last thing he wanted to do.

A stagehand told them they were ready to resume rehearsal, so he shook off his worry and went back to directing the show.

"Stand by, Rosita," Buster called. "And . . . action!"

Wearing green makeup and an unflattering green costume, Rosita was supposed to be an alien from a distant planet.

"Okay!" Buster said. "Music!"

Music started, and Rosita sang, bouncing up and down on a little trampoline hidden inside a crater on the alien planet set. Porsha ran in with a staff and pointed it at the stage in front of Rosita. *BOOM!* A stage explosion flashed and Rosita dropped through a trapdoor, out of sight.

"Take that, you nasty alien monster!" Porsha said in a wooden, unconvincing voice. She turned to Buster. "Did I do good?"

Buster could hardly believe how bad Porsha's acting was, but he wasn't about to tell her that. "Yeah," he managed to say. "That was . . . so good."

"Yay!" Porsha cheered. She ran over to the trapdoor and called down to Rosita. "Did you hear that? He thinks I'm awesome!" She pranced off.

Watching her go, Ash said to Gunter and Buster, "Okay, she cannot act."

"Yah," Gunter agreed. "She's a poo-poo actor."

"Shhh!" Buster said, raising a finger to his lips. He

sighed and whispered, "I know, I know. But I gotta keep Mr. Crystal happy."

In the wings, Porsha practiced her line. "Take THAT, you nasty alien monster!" Practicing did not make her delivery better. If anything, her acting seemed to be getting worse and worse.

Suki walked briskly into the theater and right up to Buster. "Excuse me, but Mr. Crystal wants to see you."

"Oh," Buster said, checking his rehearsal schedule. "I could come by this afternoon."

"He means now," Suki said firmly. *Right* now."

"Uh—kay," Buster said, following her out.

She led him into Mr. Crystal's palatial golden office. "You wanted to see me, sir?" Buster asked.

"Yes, I did," Mr. Crystal said in a friendly voice, standing by his huge desk. "Yes, I did. Come on in."

Relaxing a bit, Buster looked around. "Whoa. This place is incredible."

Chuckling, Mr. Crystal said, "Pretty great, huh? So, how's it going with Calloway?"

"Calloway?" Buster said. "It's, uh, it's good. Yeah, very good."

Mr. Crystal sat comfortably in the big leather chair behind his desk. "Right, right. Let me ask you something. What did I do to make you disrespect me?"

"What?" Buster asked, surprised. He'd thought the meeting was going well.

"You think I'm an idiot?" Mr. Crystal asked accusingly. "Some kinda bozo?"

Buster shook his head vigorously. "No! No, sir! Not at all!" Two big thugs moved forward, taking positions on either side of the koala.

"My team talked to Calloway's lawyer," Mr. Crystal snarled. "And they say he's never heard of you *or* your show."

"Really?" Buster said, pretending to be surprised. "They said that?"

BAM! Mr. Crystal slammed his fist on his desk. Buster jumped. "You lied to me!" Mr. Crystal roared.

"I didn't mean to!" Buster said. "I really thought I could get him!"

"No one makes me look like a fool!" Mr. Crystal barked. "NO ONE!"

Gulping, Buster said, "I wouldn't dream of doing that to you."

Mr. Crystal pointed menacingly to the imposing windows. They were many, many stories high up. "I swear, if you didn't have my kid in your show, you'd be outta that window by now!"

"Please, please, please," Buster begged, wringing his hands. "I'm so sorry!"

Mr. Crystal said in a threatening voice, "You'd better have Calloway by the end of next week, or so help me—"

"I will," Buster vowed. "I'll get him. I won't let you down, sir!"

The wolf leaned forward, showing his fangs. "Oh, I know you won't let me down."

Buster gathered Gunter, Ash, and Miss Crawly in a corner of the rehearsal space. "Listen up," he said. "I gotta go to Calloway's. And I gotta go right away."

"Oh, no," Miss Crawly gasped. "Please don't go there!"

Giving her a reassuring pat, Buster said, "Don't worry. I know you said he's crazy, but I'll be all right."

"Can I go with you, please?" Ash asked.

Buster hesitated. From what Miss Crawly had said, Calloway sounded dangerous. "Uh, I don't know. . . ."

"Come on!" Ash insisted. "You're gonna need me. I know everything about this guy."

71

Buster thought about it and nodded slowly. "I think you're right."

"Yes!" Ash said, overjoyed at the prospect of meeting her musical hero.

"Now listen, Gunter," Buster said, turning to the pig. "You've got to figure out the ending of this show on your own."

"On my own?" Gunter asked uncertainly. He was used to having Buster in the room while he came up with ideas.

"Yes," Buster confirmed. He turned to his faithful assistant. "Miss Crawly, I need you to take charge while I'm away."

"Yes, sir," Miss Crawly said, still not liking the idea of her boss going to that dangerous lion's house.

"You gotta bring your A game," he told her. "I'm serious. You gotta be tough."

"Yes, I gotta be tough!" Miss Crawly said.

"You gotta be firm," Buster said.

"Oh, and I gotta be firm! Yes!"

"And you cannot, I repeat, *cannot* let production fall behind, not one little bit. Is that clear?"

"YES, SIR, MR. MOON, SIR!" Miss Crawly said, snapping off a salute.

Miss Crawly was as good as her word. In no time at all, she was barking orders at the cast and crew through a bullhorn. "Mason! That volcano should have been finished yesterday!"

"We're on it, Miss Crawly," Mason answered, urging his crew to work faster.

"You'd better be!" Miss Crawly said, moving on to the show's two romantic young leads. "Meena! Darius! Take it from the top, and this time put a little juice in it, will ya?"

"I'm trying my best, Miss Crawly," Meena said meekly.

Darius looked confused. "A little juice?"

BLAM! A pair of doors flew open and Porsha strolled in. "Hey, everybody!" she chirped cheerfully.

Miss Crawly wasn't charmed. "You're two hours late for rehearsal!" she shouted through the bullhorn.

Porsha stared at the iguana. "Wait. Where's the koala? Who are you?"

"I'M IN CHARGE, THAT'S WHO!" Miss Crawly yelled through her bullhorn. "Now get your tail to Wardrobe!"

Buster and Ash carefully made their way through the bushes around Clay Calloway's house. The leaves were still splattered from the paintballs he'd fired at Miss Crawly. Arriving at a locked gate, Ash and Buster saw Clay working on his motorcycle.

"Oh my gosh!" Ash whispered. "There he is! That's him! He doesn't look so scary."

"Mr. Calloway?" Buster called to the famous songwriter.

Without even looking up from his task, Calloway bellowed, "GO AWAY!"

"No, please!" Buster implored. "We just want to talk to you for one minute. That's all."

The lion ignored them.

"We are not leaving until you talk to us!" Ash

called. Silence. "Fine!" she said. "If you're not coming over here, we're coming over to you!" They headed toward the fence.

"NO!" Clay shouted. "STAY OFF THE FENCE!"

"Don't listen to him," Ash said. She and Buster reached up and grabbed the fence to climb over it, but . . . ZZAP! An electric shock knocked them back and onto the grass!

They both lay there, unconscious.

Despite Miss Crawly's efforts, rehearsal was not going well. Flying on wires, Gunter and Porsha bumped into the set and each other. In Meena's duet with Darius, she had trouble looking like she was in love with him.

"What are you doing with your face?" Darius asked her. "Your face looks broken."

"Uh, I was falling in love?" Meena said uncertainly.

Darius shook his head. "That's not what falling in love with me looks like, Gina. I should know—I see it day after day, week after week. Let's run it again from the top."

When they finally took a break, Meena ran outside

and leaned against a wall, closing her eyes and sighing.

A voice said, "Would you like some ice cream, ma'am?"

She opened her eyes and saw a young elephant holding a tray of ice cream cones. His name was Alfonso. "Or should I say, Your Majesty?"

Meena didn't know what to make of this. She wasn't a queen!

"It's just that you look like a goddess," Alfonso explained. "And lucky for you, it's Free Ice Cream for All Goddesses Day."

"Oh," Meena said, giggling. Using his trunk, he offered her a cone. She accepted it with her own trunk. For just a moment, both their trunks were touching the ice cream cone.

"That's cherry cheesecake," Alfonso said, nodding toward her ice cream. "I make it all myself. See, my truck's right over there." He pointed to it. "Come by anytime, Your Majesty."

And just like that, Meena was in love.

Buster slowly opened his eyes and saw he was in a cozy living room lit by a log crackling in the fireplace. Ash was looking down at him.

76

"Buster? Are you okay?"

"Ash?" he said. "Where are we?" He noticed that his paws were bandaged.

"We're in Clay's house," Ash answered. "We were just discussing whether he'd consider being in our show."

Buster sat straight up. "What did he say?"

"He said no," said a deep voice.

Gasping, Buster turned around and saw Clay sitting right behind him.

"Not in a million years," Clay said.

15

"**P**lease, Mr. Calloway," Buster said. "You don't realize how much it would mean to have you in our show, and—"

"WOULD YOU STOP YOUR YAKKING?!" Clay roared, cutting Buster off. The little koala cowered, terrified by the huge, angry lion. Clay took Miss Crawly's glass eye out of his pocket and dropped it into Buster's lap. "Here. Your friend left this on my property."

Stomping out of the room, Clay grumbled, "I want you gone in the morning." He slammed the door behind him. *BAM!*

"And that's why they say never meet your heroes," Ash said ruefully.

That evening in a parking garage, where they wouldn't be bothered, Johnny tried to show Nooshy the steps from the dance battle, but he tripped and fell.

Realizing Klaus Kickenklober had ruined Johnny's confidence, Nooshy said, "Don't worry. We'll build up to it, step by step. Just forget what Klaus told you and go with the flow!"

She changed the music and started to dance. She would do a small move, and then she had Johnny copy her. As they went on and he mimicked her steps, he started to improve.

Nooshy smiled.

The next day, Klaus was shocked by how much better Johnny was dancing. He and Ryan did their dance fight, and Johnny got every step right!

"Woooo!" Nooshy cried.

"Nailed it!" Johnny said, thrilled.

Klaus looked furious. Nooshy plucked his hat off his head.

"Now, didn't you say you were gonna eat your hat?" she asked teasingly. "Well, here you go. Mmm,

79

yum-yum!" She laughed, but Klaus snatched his hat back, still angry.

In a dressing room, a seamstress named Louise fitted Meena for her costume. While Louise measured, Meena licked an ice cream cone. "Girl, that is your fourth today," Louise observed, nodding toward the treat.

"I know, I know," Meena admitted. "But I can't stop. I really want to talk to Alfonso, but when I get close, I get nervous, so I just buy another ice cream." She sighed, remembering how nice Alfonso looked when she'd bought her latest cone from him.

In his yard, Clay hammered a post into the ground. Attached to the wooden post was a sign that read BEWARE ELECTRIC FENCE.

Buster was still trying to convince Calloway to be in *Out of This World*.

"Honestly," he said, "this is going to be the greatest show I have ever made. Whoa!"

Buster flinched as Clay hurled his mallet into his

toolbox, just missing the koala. Picking up the nozzle attached to the end of a hose, Calloway growled, "Turn on that tap for me."

"The tap?" Buster said. "Oh, sure." He turned on the water without realizing Clay was pointing the hose right at him. *SPLOOSH!*

"WHAAA!" Buster yelped. The force of the water sent him rolling down a little hill and into the lake. *SPLASH!*

"Oopsie-daisy," Clay said, laughing.

Ash walked up just then, carrying mugs of tea. "Moon! You okay?"

"I'm okay!" Buster called up from the lake.

Ash offered Clay a mug. He looked puzzled. "It's tea," Ash explained. "You drink it." Growling, Clay took the mug.

Buster sloshed back up the hill. He was dripping wet but undeterred. "I promise," he said a little breathlessly, "this is going to be the most wonderful, fantastic show ever!"

Clay made a face and stared at his mug of tea. "Did you put honey in this?"

"And the ending?" Buster continued. "Oh, boy! It's gonna end with you and your song—" He stopped talking when Clay leaned down, nose to nose with him, and growled. Trembling a little, Buster said, "You don't want to do the show."

Nodding and turning away, Calloway said, "Besides, I lost my singing voice."

"Your voice sounds fine to me," Ash said. As Clay walked away, she decided to bring his biggest issue out into the open. "This is all because you lost your wife, isn't it?"

Clay stopped. Without looking back, he said, "Okay, porcupine. We're not talking about my Ruby."

"Look," Ash said, "I know she inspired so many of your songs—"

"All of my songs," Clay corrected, turning back to stare at her.

"Right," Ash said, trying to come up with the right words. "I can't imagine what it must be like to lose someone so special, but do you think this is what Ruby would've wanted for you? Out here all alone, never singing again?"

He turned away again, this time with tears in his eyes. "You don't understand," he said. "There's no rock star living here anymore."

"Clay, you just need to play again," Ash insisted.

"Your songs will bring you back. You can play again, and reconnect with—"

"No, I can't!" Clay roared, whirling on her in anger. "I haven't even heard one of my songs in over fifteen years. Ruby was everything. And I don't like honey in my tea." He poured the mug of tea on the grass and walked away.

Buster sighed. "He's not gonna change his mind."

But Ash wasn't ready to give up yet. "He will. But you should go back."

Looking surprised, Buster said, "Me? What about you?"

Watching Clay walk away, looking so sad, broke Ash's heart. "I just can't leave him like this." She picked the mug up from the grass and followed Clay.

When Buster walked back into the rehearsal space at the Crystal Tower Theater, Miss Crawly pressed a button on her bullhorn and spoke into it. "TEN-HUP!" Every member of the cast and crew came to attention like soldiers.

Buster was impressed. "Whoa."

Saluting, Miss Crawly barked, "Welcome back, Mr. Moon, sir!"

"Uh, thank you, Miss Crawly," he said. "Oh, and I have something for you." He handed her the glass eye.

"Thank you, Mr. Moon, sir!" Miss Crawly said, still speaking like a soldier.

"All right, you can ease off on the military attitude now," Buster said.

She lowered her bullhorn and spoke in her normal voice. "Oh. Oh, yes, yes."

Gunter hurried to ask the question everyone was thinking. "So, any luck wiz Clay Calloway?"

Buster frowned. "Shhh! Not yet. But if anyone can convince him, it's Ash." He crossed his fingers for luck. Then he turned to address the cast and crew. "All right, folks, tomorrow we have our first run-through, so let's get this show in tip-top shape!"

The crew had done an amazing job building the spaceship that Gunter and Porsha would use to travel from planet to planet. When it was brought onstage, the whole cast was excited and impressed. During

85

rehearsals, Buster controlled the spaceship from a desk in the audience. The rocket ship's door opened and Porsha stepped out.

"Captain's log," she said in a stilted voice. "I must take care, for I have landed on the Planet of War."

There were no two ways about it: Porsha was terrible. She looked nice, and she sang beautifully, but her acting was atrocious.

"Okay," Buster said. "Everyone take five. Porsha? Can I have a word?"

In the show's production office, Buster paced nervously while Porsha happily sipped on a smoothie. He tried to sound positive. "Porsha, I truly believe this show is close to being fantastic, maybe even perfect."

"Thank you," Porsha said, pausing from sipping her smoothie.

"Yeah, but to make it the best it can be," Buster hurried on, "I've got to make some changes."

"Uh-huh," Porsha said, wondering what this was all about.

Buster took a deep breath. This was it. He had to tell her. "I have to give the lead role back to Rosita."

86

"WHAT?" Porsha cried, her eyes and mouth opening wide in shock.

"I'm just offering you the opportunity to switch roles with—"

"You're *firing* me?" Porsha asked in disbelief.

Buster shook his head. "No, I'm not firing you—"

But Porsha was already heading out the door, crying. "Wait until my dad hears you fired me!"

"But I'm not firing you!" Buster called after her. "Please, wait!"

When Porsha got outside the office, she looked down the stairs and saw the entire crew looking up at her. "Oh. My. Gosh. You all *hate* me, don't you?" She ran down the stairs, weeping.

"No!" Buster cried. "We don't hate you! We all think you're terrific!"

"You and your stupid, stupid show can go to heck!" Porsha sobbed as she headed toward a pair of doors. Buster hurried after her. "Porsha, stop! Wait!"

WHAM. She slammed the doors in Buster's face. Everyone was stunned. He turned to face them and groaned.

"Oh, I am one dead koala," he said.

Clay sat in his bedroom, staring out the window at the trees. He heard Ash outside, playing the guitar and singing one of his songs. She sounded wonderful. Clay walked downstairs, pausing to look at pictures of his wife. Most of the photos held happy memories for him, but the last one showed Ruby sick in a wheelchair. He glanced over at a closet where the wheelchair still sat, folded up and tucked away.

Sitting on the front porch and singing, Ash heard the front door open. Without saying a word, Clay walked out and sat next to her. She stopped playing for a moment, looking at Calloway. She realized it was okay to keep going, so she strummed her guitar and resumed singing the sad song.

Clay sat there listening, his eyes filling with tears.

In his magnificent office, Mr. Crystal was watching Linda Le Bon on TV. "The hottest story today," she was saying, "is that Porsha Crystal was reportedly fired from her father's show—"

SMASH! Mr. Crystal slammed his fist into the TV screen. "He fired *my* daughter!" he roared. "My daughter!"

Porsha sat on a long couch, sobbing. Somehow

88

this made Mr. Crystal even madder. He wheeled on her. "Would you be quiet? You've embarrassed me enough!"

"But, Daddy!" Porsha howled.

"Now the whole world thinks I've got a talentless loser for a daughter!" Mr. Crystal raged. He turned to his two big henchmen. "Take her home." They led Porsha out of the office, still crying.

Mr. Crystal turned to Suki and Jerry.

"Bring me Moon," he snarled.

17

A pair of elevator doors slid open. Buster stood there a moment, facing the long walk to Mr. Crystal's office. Dreading what was coming, he slowly trudged along the corridor. He passed Jerry, who looked up from his desk to give Buster a look of utter disdain. The little koala remembered the big wolf's threat to toss him out a window. Would Mr. Crystal really do that? He didn't think so, but he couldn't be sure. He lifted his hand to knock on the door to Mr. Crystal's office—

BRRRING! His cell phone rang. It was Ash.

"Ash?" he said into his phone. "Now is not a good—"

"Moon!" she shouted joyfully. "I've got him!"

"What?" Buster cried.

"I got Calloway!" Ash said from the back of Clay's

90

motorcycle, yelling above the noise of the engine. "We're heading to Redshore City right now!"

"That's great!" Buster told her. "You may have just saved my life." He hung up, opened the door, and went into Mr. Crystal's office. The wolf was in a chair having his hair and makeup done for a TV appearance. "Mr. Crystal, I've got some great news! Clay Calloway is on his way here right now!"

Waving a hand, Mr. Crystal said, "Everybody out." Everyone except Buster left. "You fired Porsha," Mr. Crystal said in a low, menacing voice.

"No, I never fired her," Buster insisted.

"You calling her a liar?" Mr. Crystal growled.

"No, she just got it wrong, is all!" Buster explained. "I was only trying to help her do the best she could. Believe me, I just wanted to do the right thing."

Mr. Crystal got up from his chair and grabbed Buster by the throat. "The right thing to do is WHAT I TELL YOU TO DO!" He carried Buster out to the balcony.

"But I did!" Buster protested. "I delivered a great show! And Calloway! He's coming!" Mr. Crystal dangled Buster over the balcony's railing. "No! No! Stop!"

"You really think I'd let a little lowlife amateur loser like you humiliate me?" Mr. Crystal roared. "You made me look bad, so I'm gonna have to let you go!" Then he dropped Buster!

"Sir!" Jerry called from the door. Mr. Crystal turned to Jerry. Buster clung desperately to the cuff of the wolf's shirt. "I'm so sorry to bother you," Jerry went on, "but you have a live TV appearance in just a minute, so it might be better if we just put a pin in this right now."

Mr. Crystal threw Buster into his private bathroom. The koala stared at the wolf, horrified. "You nearly killed me!"

"And I'll finish the job later," Mr. Crystal promised.

BAM! He slammed the bathroom door shut. "No!" Buster yelled, pounding on the locked door. "Help! Jerry! ANYONE!"

Suddenly, the door flew open! Suki grabbed Buster and yanked him out. "Shhh! You need to get out of this city and never, ever come back! Do you understand? Never!"

"Okay, okay," Buster agreed. "I understand."

"I told you you weren't cut out for this," she said.

"He tried to kill me!" Buster cried.

The New Moon Theater troupe was thrilled to have talent scout Suki Lane in the audience for their performance. But Suki walked out halfway through it! Buster Moon, the theater's owner, tried to stop her.

Buster wanted to convince Suki to stay and see their talent. But Suki had already decided that they weren't good enough for Redshore City, the big leagues— where the best entertainers got to perform.

After an unsuccessful taxi chase that ended with the koala looking like a giant puffball, Buster returned to his office feeling utterly crushed. His dream of making it to Redshore City seemed to be over.

Nana Noodleman, a famous singer who supported their theater, found Buster hiding in his office. She encouraged him not to give up on his dream so easily. She said to try again!

Energized, Buster rounded up his cast and headed to dazzling Redshore City to audition for Suki's boss. They couldn't get in without an appointment, but they found a way . . . with disguises.

The competition was fierce! Legendary theater mogul Mr. Jimmy Crystal sat in the audience with a buzzer that he pressed to reject performers. Buster and his friends were nervous—Mr. Crystal was rejecting *everyone*! *BZZZZZT!*

Buster peeked through the curtain to see Mr. Crystal, the wolf who held their fate in his hands. Then Mr. Crystal's assistant, Jerry, called Buster's troupe to audition next. Their plan to sneak in had worked!

Buster, Johnny, Gunter, Meena, Rosita, and Ash started their song. But after only a dozen words, Mr. Crystal rejected them, too! Mr. Crystal told Jerry that he needed BIG shows and BIG ideas.

Gunter had a big idea, though—for an epic musical set in outer space! Featuring songs from renowned rock star Clay Calloway, the show—and the celebrity—captured Mr. Crystal's imagination.

Then Suki Lane entered the theater. She didn't believe that Buster's troupe could get Clay Calloway on board. Buster wanted to prove her wrong. He promised Mr. Crystal he'd get Clay to do their show.

Mr. Crystal was in! Everyone was excited—except Ash.
She was a huge fan of Clay Calloway, and knew something
Buster didn't: the star hadn't been seen in 15 years!

Not only did they have to find Clay Calloway, but they had to finish
writing and build their sets! They had just three weeks to put the
whole show together, or Mr. Crystal would be very angry. . . .

Buster gave the job of finding Clay Calloway
to his assistant, an elderly iguana named Miss Crawly.
She was eager to help with such an important task!

Miss Crawly brought a fruit basket for the reclusive rock star.
But Clay did not want any visitors—as Miss Crawly soon learned
from his extensive security! She didn't even get to meet him.

Back in Redshore City, Buster was in trouble. Mr. Crystal had learned that Clay Calloway had never heard of Buster or his show! The koala had to come through with Clay . . . or else!

Buster and Ash went to find the rock star. Would they be able to persuade him to join their show—and perform for the first time in 15 years?

"Yeah," Suki said. "And when he finds you're gone, he'll have his thugs looking all over town for you."

"Okay. Thank you, Suki," Buster told her. "I'm so—"

"Get outta here!" Suki barked.

Buster ran out of Mr. Crystal's office. Once he was on the street, he ran for his life. As he ran, he called Miss Crawly on his phone. "Get out!" he told her. "All of you! Get out of there right now! There's no time to explain. Just get the cast and meet me back at the hotel. Whoa!" He bumped into a pedestrian and his phone went flying into the street, where a bus ran over it.

CRUNCH.

18

On a different floor of the skyscraper, Mr. Crystal stood waiting to be a guest on a TV show that covered showbiz news. "Jerry!" he called to his weary assistant. "Go get my snacks!"

"Yes, sir!" Jerry said, hurrying off. When he sprinted into Mr. Crystal's office, he noticed the open door to the bathroom. Gasping, he realized Buster had escaped!

Back in the TV studio, the news host, Linda Le Bon, was introducing Mr. Crystal to the audience in the auditorium. "And now, here to discuss the drama surrounding his new show, Mr. Redshore City himself . . ."

Jerry rushed up to Mr. Crystal, still waiting in the wings. "Sir!" The cat gestured for the wolf to bend down so he could whisper the bad news of Buster's escape in his ear.

"What?" Mr. Crystal barked, enraged at the update.

". . . please welcome . . . Mr. Jimmy Crystal!" Linda Le Bon announced. Music played. Backstage, a crew member frantically gestured for Mr. Crystal to enter. "Come on out here, Jimmy!" Le Bon said. "Don't make us beg!"

Snapping his fingers, Mr. Crystal summoned his two big thugs. "Moon got out," he told them. "Find him." They nodded and rushed away.

Stalling, Linda Le Bon smiled at her live audience. "Does this guy know how to make an entrance or what?"

Mr. Crystal plastered on a big fake smile and strode onto the stage. "Hey, everybody!" he said, laughing. "Good to see you! Linda! I got some hot news for you—you look terrific!" The audience cheered and applauded.

In his hotel suite, Buster frantically stuffed clothes into his suitcase. Then . . . *DING-DONG! KNOCK, KNOCK!* Someone was at the door. Mr. Crystal's goons

95

had found him! He yanked all the clothes out of the suitcase, climbed in, and zipped it closed.

Buster heard the door open. He held his breath. Footsteps approached.

"Buster?" said a voice.

It was Ash!

"Ash!" Buster called from inside the suitcase. "In here!"

Ash and Clay stared at the suitcase as it wobbled around. "Buster?" Ash repeated.

"I'm stuck!" Buster explained, straining to escape from the baggage.

"You gotta be kidding me," Clay said.

Ash tried to unzip the bag. "Hold still," she said, tugging at the zipper. "What are you doing in there?"

"Ash, the show's off," Buster explained. "Mr. Crystal got mad and tried to kill me."

"What?" Ash exclaimed.

Buster tumbled out of the bag and onto the floor. *THUD!* "I thought you were Mr. Crystal's thugs coming to finish me off," he explained, a little out of breath.

DING-DONG! KNOCK, KNOCK!

"Oh, no!" Buster whispered frantically. "It's them!

96

Shhh! Pretend we're not here." He started to climb back into the suitcase.

The doorbell rang again. *DING-DONG!* Unconcerned, Clay spoke in a perfectly normal voice. "Hmm. First time I leave home in fifteen years, and what do I find? The show is off, and this guy's hiding in a suitcase." He walked over to the door.

"No! No!" Buster whispered. "Don't open the door!"

Clay opened it. Rosita, Meena, Johnny, Nooshy, Gunter, and Miss Crawly all gasped, then cried, "Clay Calloway!" He leaned over, studying Miss Crawly. Scowling, he said, "Hmm. I remember you."

The iguana fainted clean away, falling to the floor in a heap. *THUMP!*

Moments later, Miss Crawly came to in a chair. Buster was urging her to get stand. "Miss Crawly, wake up! We gotta get out of here." He helped her from the chair.

"Coast is clear," Johnny said, checking the hall. "Let's go!"

"Come on, Miss Crawly," Meena urged. "Come on."

"We'll all feel better when we're safe at home," Buster said.

"You sure about that?" Clay said, looking at their sad faces. "Because I can tell you, running and hiding away isn't all it's cracked up to be."

Buster looked at Clay in disbelief. Hadn't he heard what Buster had said about Mr. Crystal trying to kill him? "Well," he said, "we don't have a choice."

Clay nodded. "Yeah, well, all these years, I thought the same. But it turns out, there's always a choice. I just never had the guts to make the right one. You know what I mean?"

Buster thought about it. Then he heard Mr. Crystal talking on the TV in the room.

"My Porsha was a victim in all this. I shut down my show because of a talentless little twerp named Buster Moon," Mr. Crystal was telling the audience. "You should have seen this teeny-tiny loser and his pathetic, amateur friends. Whatever Podunk town they crawled out of, that's where they belong, not in this great city!"

CLICK. Buster turned off the TV with the remote. He looked at his friends, all looking hurt and disappointed. Thinking hard, he said, "No. See, Clay's right. What we're trying to do here takes guts. We cannot let that bully steal our hopes and dreams."

"No, no," Rosita protested. "We are *way* past singing and dancing now."

"Look, I know this might sound crazy," Buster said. "But if we got the theater back, just for one night . . ."

Johnny looked skeptical. "Oh, come on, seriously? It's not like we can just sneak in there and put the show on behind Mr. Crystal's back!"

There was silence for a moment. Then, with a determined look on his face, Buster said, "That is exactly what we're going to do!"

19

The cast members stood there, astonished by Buster's bold statement. Then they started to grin and nod.

"Yes!" Nooshy exclaimed, pumping a fist.

DING-DONG!

Everyone froze. "Maybe it's room service?" Gunter suggested.

DING-DONG! BAM! BAM! BAM! BAM!

"Open up or you're dead, Moon!" threatened a deep voice from the other side of the door.

"Okay, it's not room service," Gunter admitted.

BAM! BAM! BAM! BAM!

"YOU AND YOUR DUMB FRIENDS BETTER NOT BE HIDING IN THERE!" the voice shouted. The thugs pounded on the door again. *BAM! BAM! BAM!*

Trembling with fear, Meena asked, "What are we going to do?"

"Guys, we just gotta be brave now," Buster told them.

"Are you saying we should fight these thugs?" Johnny asked, wishing he had his stick from the show's battle dance.

"No, no," Buster said, shaking his head. "They'll beat us to a pulp."

BAM! BAM! The door started to buckle. Everybody gasped!

"We're gonna put on this show whether Mr. Crystal likes it or not," Buster said determinedly. "But first, we're gonna jump out that window!" He pointed to the room's big window.

"What?" they all cried.

Clay smiled. "I'm beginning to like this guy."

BAM! BAM! CRASH!

The two thugs broke down the door with a fire extinguisher. They rushed into the room just in time to see Buster and his friends leap off the room's balcony into the hotel pool below! *SPLOOSH! SPLASH! SPLORSH!* Sputtering and gasping, they surfaced, and then were surprised to be swept off by a current!

Speaking into the microphone on his headset, one thug said, "Security? We got nine suspects loose on the River Ride. Repeat, nine suspects loose on the River Ride." The hotel pool, it turned out, was connected to the rapidly flowing River Ride.

WHOOOOSH! The cast members were pulled along through the rapids. "Hang on, everybody!" Buster yelled. They all clung to their luggage, coursing through a fake jungle.

At the end of the ride, two guards searched for the suspects. Puzzled, one of them said into his walkie-talkie, "This is Pool Security. I don't see anyone here. Over."

Then the other guard spotted them on a security camera. "There!" he cried. "They're heading through the back lot!"

Dripping wet, the performers scrambled through the fake jungle undergrowth.

"Go, go, go!" Buster cried, urging them on.

Dragging his suitcase, Gunter said, "I wish I didn't have such teeny-tiny legs right now!"

When Miss Crawly collapsed from exhaustion, Clay Calloway picked her up and carried her without missing a step. They all reached a wall at the edge of the property, climbed over it, and ran down the street. By the time the security guards reached the area, the friends were gone.

Smiling and waving goodbye to the audience, Mr. Crystal walked off the set of Linda Le Bon's show. "Thank you, Linda! Thank you! Thanks, everybody!" The audience applauded loudly.

As soon as Mr. Crystal reached backstage, he dropped his smile. Jerry handed him a phone, and he lifted it to his ear. "Well?" he growled.

"No sign of 'em, sir," one of the thugs reported from a bus stop. "We think they might've split town." Mr. Crystal threw the phone. It hit the floor and smashed into pieces. *CRASH!*

Mr. Crystal stormed off, furious.

Buster led the way as the cast rushed down an alley next to the theater. Using a key card to unlock the door, they slipped into the theater and switched on the lights. They gasped! Two hundred big eyes were staring at them!

103

The eyes belonged to a cleaning crew of one hundred tarsiers—furry little creatures with huge eyes and long tails, looking a bit like wingless bats or big-eared monkeys.

"No one is supposed to be in here," one of the tarsiers said.

"Uh, who are you?" Buster asked.

"We're the night cleaners," the tarsier explained.

"Oh, I see," Buster replied. "Well, we don't need any cleaning right now. But it'd be better if you didn't leave, so . . . I don't suppose any of you can tap-dance, can you?"

The tarsiers looked at each other in disbelief. But then one of them raised a hand.

"Ah!" Buster said, pleased. He turned to his cast. "Well, let's move it, folks!" They all grabbed their costumes and props. Buster handed Rosita her space helmet. "Here, Rosita," he said. "It's your role." She hugged the helmet, beaming with joy.

"Miss Crawly," Buster said. "Let's see if we can get us a new green alien."

"Yes sir, Mr. Moon, sir!" she answered, snapping to attention.

Porsha lay on her bed at home, sobbing. Outside her window, Miss Crawly appeared with her bullhorn. "RISE AND SHINE, SWEETHEART!"

In no time at all, Porsha and Miss Crawly were back at the theater. Buster turned and saw them. "Hey! You made it!"

"Yeah," Porsha said sheepishly. "Maybe I overreacted a little before."

Gunter overheard. "A little? You were like a total drama queen back there!"

"Yeah, okay," Buster said, smoothing things over. "We're all good now."

Porsha shook her head. "Wow, my dad's gonna flip when he hears about us putting on the show in his theater without his permission."

"Well, we're safe for now," Buster said optimistically.

But Porsha knew her father better than that. "Safe?" she repeated, laughing. "No. None of us are safe."

Johnny joined the conversation. "Mr. Moon? I know someone who can protect us."

105

20

Johnny placed a quick call to his father, Big Daddy, asking if he and his fellow gorillas could provide protection.

"Say no more, son," Big Daddy assured him. "We're on our way." He gathered his guys, climbed into their truck, and roared off, bound for Redshore City.

Backstage at the Crystal Tower Theater, the cast members were getting ready to put on *Out of This World*. Dancers snuck in the back door. Ash tuned her guitar. The tarsiers rehearsed their tap dance. Porsha tried on the green alien costume. Johnny airbrushed war paint onto his face. Rosita put on her makeup.

In his lavish personal bathroom, Mr. Crystal was getting ready for bed. Wearing a bathrobe, he brushed his long, sharp teeth to a gleaming polish and admired them in the mirror. Perfect!

Exiting the bathroom, he walked through his luxurious bedroom, opened the door, and leaned out into the hallway. He looked toward Porsha's bedroom and saw a light shining from under the door.

"Good night, Porsha," he called to her coldly.

He had no idea that Porsha's room was empty.

He stood there a moment, waiting for his daughter to respond. When he heard nothing, he growled, "All right—be that way! I don't care!" Then he muttered under his breath, "Spoiled little brat."

Mr. Crystal stepped back into his bedroom and slammed the door. *WHAM!*

Back in the theater, Buster walked outside the dressing rooms, checking to make sure everything was all right. After he'd assured himself that everyone had the costumes, props, and makeup they needed for *Out of This World*, he nodded and said, "Okay, time to get us an audience!"

107

Ash looked worried. "Moon, as soon as you start inviting people in here, hotel security will shut us down!"

But Buster looked confident. "Oh, it's okay," he assured her. "Rosita's got that covered. He pointed to Rosita, who spoke into her phone.

"Norman," she said, "release the piglets."

Norman led all their children to the Crystal Tower Hotel buffet and let them run wild! When they saw the food spread out on the tables for the all-you-can-eat buffet, they went crazy, squealing and running everywhere, eating to their hearts' content. A few employees tried to chase the little piglets and catch them, but they were way too fast, easily escaping.

A security guard chased one piglet down the length of a buffet table that was covered with food. Watching in horror, the restaurant host desperately called a number on his phone.

"ALL SECURITY!" he gasped. "WE HAVE A SITUATON ON FLOOR SEVENTEEN! I REPEAT, ALL SECURITY TO FLOOR SEVENTEEN!"

A girl piglet named Candy swam in a chocolate fountain, squealing, "THIS IS THE BEST DAY OF MY LIFE, DADDY!" Norman grinned. She jumped out of the fountain just before a guard tried to grab her. He slipped and landed facedown in the chocolate. *BLORSH!*

Down in the huge hotel lobby, all the security guards scrambled into the elevators, rushing to the seventeenth floor. As soon as they were gone, a huge TV screen turned on, and Buster addressed the guests in the lobby.

"Good evening! My name is Buster Moon, and it is my great pleasure to present to you, for one night only, in the Crystal Tower Theater . . ."

Everyone in the lobby turned to watch Buster's announcement, including a concerned concierge, who immediately called Jerry.

". . . a brand-new show called *Out of This World*!" Buster's voice boomed all over the building, as well as outside, where people were enjoying Alfonso's ice cream cones.

As soon as Jerry got the call, he ran to tell Mr. Crystal. In the lobby, Klaus Kickenklober heard Buster's announcement and raced toward the theater's backstage to see what in the world was going on.

"A musical space odyssey featuring the return of the legendary Clay Calloway!" Buster continued.

The people watching the building's TV screens were thrilled when they heard the news about Calloway. "That's right—Clay Calloway! And what's more, this show is completely FREE! So step right up and take your seats! The journey of a lifetime is about to begin!"

Excitement crackled through the building. A free show! Clay Calloway! People rushed into the theater and filled the seats.

Backstage, Buster asked, "All right, everybody. We all set back here?"

The stage doors opened, and a huge gorilla entered with his arms open wide. "There he is!" he said, spotting his son.

"Dad!" Johnny called, running to hug him. Behind Big Daddy were several more gorillas, ready to do whatever was necessary to protect Johnny's show.

Peeking through the curtain, Meena gasped, "Oh my gosh! He's here!"

"Mr. Crystal's here?" Buster asked, terrified.

"No," Meena clarified. "My ice cream guy. And he's sitting in the front row!"

110

BAM! The door to the private living quarters in Mr. Crystal's mansion flew open and Jerry rushed in.

"Mr. Crystal! Mr. Crystal!" the cat called frantically.

"I tried to stop him, sir," said one of Mr. Crystal's thugs.

"I'm so sorry to interrupt, sir," Jerry said. "But it's Moon. He's taken over the theater, and he's putting on a show right now!"

"HE'S *WHAAAAAT*?" Mr. Crystal roared.

21

In the auditorium, the lights dimmed. The audience murmured, excited to see a brand-new show with Clay Calloway in it. They started to clap in rhythm.

Big Daddy and his gang roamed the aisles, protecting the show.

Backstage, Buster addressed the whole cast. "Okay, this is it, guys. You ready?"

Putting their arms around each other's shoulders, the actors formed a big group hug.

"Oh my gosh," Rosita said. "Are we really doing this?"

"Yeah, you better believe it!" Johnny said enthusiastically.

"YAH!" Gunter exclaimed. "Big-time, baby!"

From inside the group hug, Buster told them,

"Remember, there's only one way left to go, and that's UP!" Full of excited energy, the cast broke out of the huddle and took their positions for the start of the show.

Moving stiffly for his robot role, Gunter said, "Gunter robot activating piggy power! *Beep! Beep! Boop! Boop!*"

Settling into his stage manager's spot backstage, Buster pointed at Miss Crawly and said, "Playback!" She hit a button, and music began to play. Now Buster leaned toward a microphone. "All creatures great and small," he said, "welcome to outer space!"

Stars lit the stage. A huge rocket ship with a glass front lowered into view. Through the glass, the audience could see Rosita standing on the control deck.

"Captain's log," she said. "My mission: to find and rescue a space explorer who mysteriously went missing long ago."

Sprayed with silver paint to make him look like a robot, Gunter entered the deck. "Captain! I am picking up his signal!"

Rosita turned toward Gunter. "Excellent! But from which planet? I see four of them ahead."

"It is impossible to know which one the signal is

coming from," Gunter said in his robot voice.

"I see," Rosita said, turning back to gaze out the front of the spaceship. "Then I'll have to explore them all. Take us down!"

As the rocket lowered onto the stage, Johnny waited to make his entrance. Looking out at the huge audience, he suddenly felt very nervous.

"You've got this, big guy!" Nooshy reassured him, patting his shoulder. "Remember what I said: just go with the flow." Johnny nodded, took a deep breath, and walked out onstage.

From the deck of the ship, Rosita said, "Captain's log. I must take care, for I have landed on the Planet of War." The set looked like a futuristic town ruined by battle, with broken buildings, torn flags, and small fires.

As Johnny began to sing, his dad watched proudly.

"That's my boy," he said softly.

With one last look at Nooshy in the wings for inspiration, Johnny began to dance.

And he danced magnificently! The audience clapped and cheered!

The other dancers waited eagerly to go onstage. Looking angry, Klaus stomped over to Ryan. "Give me that stick," he demanded, "and your costume. Now!"

"Wait, what?" Ryan said, baffled by the choreographer's order.

"TAKE IT OFF," Klaus barked. "NOW!"

"Faster!" Mr. Crystal ordered from the back seat of a long limousine racing through the streets of Redshore City. In the limo with him were Jerry, Suki, and the two hulking thugs.

"Uh, we'll be at the theater soon, sir," the limo driver said.

"I don't wanna be there soon," Mr. Crystal snarled. "I wanna be there now!"

"Yeah, we wanna be there now," Jerry echoed.

"Yes, sir," the driver said, flooring it. *VROOOOM!* Everyone was pinned to their seats by the force of the speeding car.

Onstage, Johnny was joined by his fellow dancers. He looked for Ryan, but was surprised to see Klaus, in costume, twirling Ryan's fighting stick. The sight of the nasty choreographer made Johnny nervous, but he

115

pulled out his own fighting stick, ready to accept the challenge.

In the center of the stage, right in front, Klaus and Johnny performed their battle dance. But Klaus seemed to be treating it as a real battle, hitting Johnny with the stick instead of just missing him, like he was supposed to. The more Klaus mocked and taunted Johnny, the angrier Johnny got and the more mistakes he made, until finally, he slipped and fell. Klaus pinned Johnny to the ground with his stick and stood over him.

"You see?" he whispered, grinning evilly. "You will never be great, Johnny!"

22

Klaus bowed to the cheering audience, which thought it was all part of the show. Johnny looked offstage and saw Nooshy and his dad looking desperate. Nooshy got an idea. She hurried over to a barrel backstage and started pounding on it rhythmically. The other dancers joined her rhythm, pounding their sticks on the stage. Inspired, Johnny got to his feet, pounding his stick, singing, facing off against Klaus.

The choreographer lunged at Johnny, but the gorilla dodged him and danced to the rhythm of the pounding sticks, spinning like a whirlwind all around the stage.

"Yeah, that's more like it," Nooshy said as she watched proudly.

Johnny danced around Klaus, completely letting

himself go, following the beat. The crowd went crazy for his phenomenal dancing! Even Klaus was filled with awe watching Johnny move. His eyes filled with tears.

When the song ended, Klaus dropped his stick and knelt before Johnny, looking up and nodding his approval. Johnny just stood there, breathing hard. The audience exploded with applause and cheers!

Johnny smiled.

Backstage, Buster whooped and laughed, hugging Nooshy.

But then the voice of one of the gorillas came over Big Daddy's walkie-talkie. "This is Barry. Come in. Over."

Big Daddy pressed a button on his walkie-talkie and spoke into it quietly. "Yeah, go ahead, Barry."

From outside, near the grand entrance to the hotel, Barry reported, "Mr. Crystal's on-site. Repeat. Mr. Crystal is on-site. Over."

"Roger that," Big Daddy said. "Over." He cracked his knuckles. "All right, let's go to work."

Onstage, Rosita stepped out of the spaceship. "Captain's log," she said. "The missing explorer was not on the Planet of War. So my search has brought me to the second planet: the Planet of Joy."

From his workstation, Buster spoke into his headset. "All right, Porsha, here we go. Time to show the world what you're really made of."

POW! Onstage, Porsha was launched out of a crater. She landed right next to Rosita, wearing the green alien costume that had briefly been Rosita's. On Porsha, the costume looked great! Singing in her beautiful voice, Porsha walked up to an angry inflatable alien rising out of a crater behind Rosita. She poked her claw into the alien, and . . . *POP!* Golden glitter fell, revealing a happy inflatable alien to replace the angry one. Still singing, Porsha worked her way around the stage, popping angry aliens and turning them into happy ones. *POP! POP! POP!*

Out in the lobby, Mr. Crystal and his thugs ran up, only to be met by Big Daddy and his gorillas.

"Who the heck are you?" Mr. Crystal demanded. "Where's my security?"

"We're security now, mate," Big Daddy replied calmly.

"What?" Mr. Crystal said. He gestured toward the gorillas, and his thugs attacked. *WHAM! WHAP!*

BAM! While they fought, Mr. Crystal slipped away, heading for the theater's backstage.

Meanwhile, Porsha kept singing, dancing among the rainbow-colored inflatable aliens swaying in time with the music while Rosita looked on. She was enchanted—and so was the audience. Porsha's singing was delightful!

But from backstage, Mr. Crystal hissed at his daughter. "Porsha! Get off of there!"

The audience couldn't hear the wolf, but Porsha could. She shook her head at him, refusing to leave the stage.

"Don't you make me come out there!" Mr. Crystal warned her. She kept singing. And behind her, stars in the sky flipped around to reveal the one hundred tarsiers dressed in top hats and tuxedos! They tap-danced around Porsha as she gracefully danced all over the set.

"You traitor!" Mr. Crystal called accusingly. "That's it! I'm coming out there!" But when he took a step forward, Buster yanked a lever, opening a trapdoor. *CLONK!* Mr. Crystal fell into a small chamber beneath the stage. Buster moved to the edge of the open door and peered down at the furious wolf.

"Miss Crawly put some cushions and snacks down there, so you should be comfortable until the show's over," Buster told him.

Mr. Crystal seethed. "You little—"

SLAM! Buster closed the trapdoor.

23

With the tarsiers tap-dancing their hearts out behind her, Porsha, as a joyful green alien, built to the big finish of her song. The tarsiers formed a pyramid with Porsha at the top. When she ended her last note, the applause was like a thunderclap! She held her pose, smiling, taking it all in.

"Captain's log," Rosita said when the clapping had finally stopped, "no sign of the missing space explorer here on the Planet of Joy. We will proceed to the Planet of Love."

Backstage, Meena and Darius waited to make their entrance. The music for their love duet began to play.

"Ready, Gina?" Darius asked.

"It's Meena," she told him for the hundredth time, a bundle of nerves. She was also exasperated.

"Wait," Darius said, confused. "What is?"

Trembling, Meena took a deep breath. "Never mind."

"Listen, find that romantic feeling," Darius advised the young elephant. "It is now or never."

Desperate to feel the mood of the song, Meena looked out at the audience. She saw Alfonso sitting in the front row. When she turned back to Darius, she closed her eyes tightly, imagining he was Alfonso. And when she opened her eyes, she saw Alfonso standing right there in front of her, wearing his ice cream uniform! Grinning with delight at her imaginary partner, Meena said, "Okay. I'm ready now."

Onstage, Rosita stood beside the spaceship, peering through high-tech binoculars. Meena waltzed onto the stage, dancing with Alfonso (in her mind) through an enchanted alien forest as they sang their duet. Partway through the song, she dropped her cloak, revealing that she was wearing a magnificent long white dress. As she danced, twirling and spinning, the dress billowed around her.

But she wasn't the only one spinning. Out in the lobby, Big Daddy sent one of Mr. Crystal's thugs spinning across the floor past Jerry, who was answering his phone.

"Mr. Crystal!" he said, surprised. "Where are you?"

"I'm trapped somewhere under the stage!" Mr. Crystal shouted, rattling the door of his cage.

"I'll find you, sir!" Jerry promised before hanging up. Screwing his eyes shut, the cat dashed through the battling gorillas and thugs, making his way toward the theater. Running blind, he somehow managed to dodge all the flying fists and feet! It helped that he was considerably smaller than the bulky combatants.

Moments later, Suki entered the lobby and was stunned to see a dozen security guards and both of Mr. Crystal's thugs lying on the ground, dazed and defeated. Big Daddy was wiping his hands together, pleased with a job well done.

Onstage, Meena and Darius (who was still

Alfonso in her mind) rode the planet's rotating rings, separating and then coming back together as they sang their duet. Then they rushed from the rings and through a tunnel of flowers to the front of the stage. They finished their song in a romantic pose, and the audience went wild, whooping and clapping!

Smiling a huge smile, Meena turned to her imaginary Alfonso and saw him turn back into Darius. He let go of her hand and strutted across the stage, soaking up the applause. "Yes! I am going to win a *ton* of awards for this!" he crowed.

Meena looked down at the real Alfonso, sitting in a front-row seat just a few feet from her. As the rocket ship took off behind her, covering the sound of her voice, she said, "Hi!"

"Uh, hi," Alfonso answered, surprised at being spoken to directly by a performer on the stage.

"I'm Meena," she finally managed to tell him.

"Oh. Um. Alfonso," he replied. "You were incredible."

"So were you," Meena said.

The elephant looked confused. "Um . . . what?"

"Oh, uh, never mind," Meena said. "Um, wanna meet up after the show, maybe?"

"Uh, okay," Alfonso agreed, smiling warmly.

Meena grinned. "Okay, great! Bye!"

She exited the stage practically floating on air—which isn't easy for an elephant.

24

The spaceship lowered back into view. The audience could see Rosita and Gunter through its glass front.

Sitting at a control panel, robot Gunter twisted in his seat to address Rosita. "Captain!" he said in a robotic version of his accented voice. "Ve cannot land on ze last planet!"

"Why not?" Rosita asked.

"Zere is, like, a huge vormhole!" Gunter explained. "The ship will never make it."

"You're right," she said, picking up her space helmet. "The ship won't make it. But I will."

Music began. Rosita and Gunter danced as she sang a song about going for your goals, no matter how dangerous the task at hand might be.

Under the stage, Jerry used a crowbar to release

Mr. Crystal from his cage. "Watch your fingers," he warned.

WHAM! Mr. Crystal impatiently shoved the door open, which sent Jerry flying back. Panting and boiling with rage, Mr. Crystal rushed out of the cage, intent upon finding Buster. And punishing him.

Onstage, Rosita danced out of the spaceship and onto the diving board that had terrified her before. When she reached the edge of the board, she looked down and saw how far it was to the stage. Breathing fast, she stopped singing and backed up until she was in the spaceship again.

"Rosita?" Gunter whispered. "You've got to jump!"

From the audience, Norman could see his wife's fear. "Oh, honey," he said softly.

Backstage, sitting at the soundboard, Buster muttered, "Come on, Rosita. . . ."

Suddenly, Meena shrieked, "Look out!"

Her warning came too late. Mr. Crystal grabbed Buster by the collar and lifted him out of his chair. Cast and crew members immediately surrounded Mr. Crystal, including his daughter.

"Daddy!" Porsha cried. "Stop it!"

Before they could rescue Buster, Mr. Crystal

stepped back onto an elevator platform, hit a switch, and shot up toward the catwalk high above the stage.

"Mr. Moon!" Miss Crawly called.

"Noooo!" Meena wailed.

The platform stopped one hundred feet above the stage. "Well, I've got you now, you lowlife little loser," Mr. Crystal snarled, gripping Buster tightly in his claws as he stepped off the elevator onto the catwalk.

Buster looked the wolf right in the eye. "No, sir, I'm not a loser. We did what we came here to do, and there is nothing you can do or say to change that."

Mr. Crystal's face twisted with rage. "Oh, I can do whatever I want." And with that, Mr. Crystal tossed Buster into the air, sending him plummeting toward the stage below! Terrified, Buster flailed with his arms and legs as he fell!

When Rosita saw Buster being thrown, she ran off the diving board without hesitating for a second. She flew through the air on a wire . . . and CAUGHT BUSTER! He opened his eyes and was astonished to find himself in her arms. After depositing him on a raised platform backstage, Rosita swung back out over the audience, singing right in time to the music.

The cast members backstage were thrilled! Johnny gave Miss Crawly a big hug.

Onstage, Gunter followed Rosita, leaping off the rocket ship and soaring joyously through the air. They flew in magnificent loops around the rainbow-colored stage and out over the audience.

Furious, Mr. Crystal turned back to the elevator platform, planning to ride it to the stage and get his claws on Buster again. But the elevator was gone! It had been called back down by Suki, who'd had enough of her boss's violent ways. Mr. Crystal was stuck up on the catwalk high above the stage with no way to get down. And then he felt a huge hand on his shoulder. He turned and found himself staring into the eyes of Big Daddy. The gorilla grinned.

Rosita and Gunter landed in a spotlight at center stage and struck a heroic pose, then went into a terrific dance routine.

"WOOO!" Gunter yelled. "OH, BABY!"

When the song ended, the audience went wild, breaking into thunderous applause and cheers. Norman and the piglets whistled and whooped for Rosita.

"Woo-hoo!" Norman called to his wife. "I love you!"

Backstage, Miss Crawly, Meena, Nooshy, and

Johnny were celebrating. Buster joined them.

"Oh, Mr. Moon," Miss Crawly said, concerned. "Are you okay?"

"Yeah, never better," Buster said, smiling. "Where are Ash and Clay?"

In a private corner backstage, Clay opened his guitar case for the first time in fifteen years. Inside, he found a picture of his wife, Ruby. The sight reawakened his pain of losing her, and he shut the case.

Ash rushed up to him. "Clay? Clay? You back here? We're on next!"

He walked toward Ash, lost in thought.

"You okay?" Ash asked.

"Uh-huh," Clay said flatly.

Onstage, Rosita and Gunter walked up to the mouth of a beautiful crystal cave. Rosita said her line: "Captain's log. We have survived the wormhole and arrived on the last planet. The missing space explorer must be here somewhere, but there's no sign of life on my scanner."

At the backstage entrance to the cave set, Ash said anxiously, "That's your cue." But Clay just stood there, saying nothing. "Clay, it's time to go on."

"But I see no signs of life," Rosita said onstage,

stalling for time. "Nothing but an empty cave."

Clay started panting anxiously.

"Clay?" Ash said. "It's okay."

"Oh, no," Clay said, rooted to the spot. Ash could see that he was in pain.

"Just sing," she gently coaxed. "Your songs will carry you."

He shook his head. "No, this is a mistake."

"Please," Ash pleaded.

"It's been so long," Clay said. "I'm not ready. I'm sorry, but I'm not ready."

25

Gunter and Rosita stared at the mouth of the crystal cave, not sure what to do. Then Ash stepped out of the cave, singing one of Clay Calloway's old songs alone. Buster and Clay watched from backstage as Ash turned to the audience and lifted her hands while she sang . . .

. . . and everyone in the audience started singing with her! They all knew and loved Clay's song, remembering every word and note.

When Clay heard the whole audience singing his song, his eyes filled with tears. He lifted his guitar and began to play.

The second that the audience heard his guitar, they cheered, whooped, and clapped. And as Clay Calloway walked out of the crystal cave, playing and singing, they leapt to their feet, excited and thrilled.

Ash and Clay sang the song together. Clay smiled at Ash, grateful to her for encouraging him to play and sing again. From his place at the soundboard, Buster felt overjoyed.

The song reached its climax, and the audience joined in again. Everyone in the theater sang together. Ash's costume lit up, and the effect spread across the stage as she, Clay, Gunter, and Rosita rose toward the spaceship. On the last note of the song, Rosita said, "Mission accomplished. We're heading home."

The song ended to the loudest applause of the night. The audience gave the cast a standing ovation, stomping their feet and clapping with all their might. Norman and the piglets squealed with delight. Clay looked out at the crowd, smiling. It felt good to be back.

Backstage, Big Daddy shoved Mr. Crystal along to the bottom of the stairs that led down from the catwalk. The cast lined up for their curtain call, and beckoned for Buster to join them. He did, walking right past Mr. Crystal.

The cast took curtain call after curtain call,

bowing again and again. The audience didn't want to let them leave. It was an incredibly magical night.

Backstage, Mr. Crystal was speechless, amazed by the crowd's reaction to the show. Linda Le Bon rushed up to him. "Jimmy! Listen to that crowd! You're a genius!"

Always quick to agree when his boss got a compliment, Jerry said, "Yeah, you really are a genius, sir!"

Mr. Crystal slowly realized that he could take credit for the show's success and get away with it. "Yeah," he said. "You got that right, Linda."

The cast was taking one last bow. When they stood up, they were surprised to see Mr. Crystal standing on the stage in front of them, smiling at the audience, holding up his hands for them to quiet down.

"Thank you, thank you," he said. "Too kind. I appreciate it. Really, I do. Look, I am very proud of this show. We did great work here, great work. And my good friend, Clay. Great to have him back, right? Yeah. And listen, I look forward to seeing this show run at my theater for many, many years to come. Right, Moon?"

He turned and was surprised to see that the cast had left. He was all alone on the stage. The audience began to laugh.

"Moon?" he repeated.

The laughter built. Embarrassed, Mr. Crystal looked to the wings for help and saw six police officers standing next to Suki.

She pointed at Mr. Crystal and said, "Officers, arrest that wolf."

As the police officers marched toward Mr. Crystal, Jerry ran after them, pleading, "No! Stop! He's innocent!" Jerry was true to his boss till the bitter end.

On the bus out of Redshore City, Buster and the cast members took one last look out the windows at the shining hotels, theme parks, fountains, and monorails, savoring the sights of the town where they'd succeeded so thoroughly.

Sharing headphones, Johnny and Nooshy waved at Big Daddy as he drove past the bus in his truck. Gunter sat beside Meena, who was on a video call with Alfonso. The screen of her phone was covered in heart emojis. Ash dozed, leaning her head on Clay's shoulder. The piglets slept next to Miss Crawly. Buster sat with Porsha. They turned and looked out the bus's back window at a sign that read GOODBYE FROM REDSHORE CITY.

TAP! TAP! TAP! Someone was tapping on the window. They looked and saw Suki riding a moped!

"STOP THE BUS!" she shouted.

SCREECH! Everyone lurched forward as the bus braked. Suki hurried up the steps of the bus and stood in the aisle. "I just got a call from the Majestic," she said, a little out of breath. "They think your show is fantastic, and they want to put it on at their theater!"

Everyone cheered!

On the opening night of *Out of This World* at the Majestic, a long, fancy car pulled up to the red carpet in front of the entrance. The driver opened the door for Nana Noodleman, who was dressed up for the occasion. Members of the press took her picture. Wearing a tuxedo and bursting with pride, Buster offered Nana his arm and escorted her into the theater for the big premiere.

137

Backstage, the cast took their places on the stage behind the curtain, ready to perform. Nana blew them a good-luck kiss as she passed through.

Buster led her to a box seat in the balcony, where they joined Miss Crawly, Norman, Alfonso, and Hobbs. They all sat down, eager for the curtain to rise and the show to begin.

But Buster was too excited to stay in his seat. He hopped down and leaned over the balcony rail, gazing at the packed house in joy and wonder. They'd actually done it! They'd hit the big time! Their dream had come true!

The curtain rose, and the show began.